CHRISTMAS COOKIES AND CRIMINALS

A CHOCOLATE CENTERED COZY MYSTERY

CINDY BELL

CONTENTS

ISBN: 9781671728394

CHAPTER 1

The ding of the bell over the door startled Ally Sweet. She had turned the sign in the window of Charlotte's Chocolate Heaven to open, then hurried back to the kitchen to start another batch of chocolate crinkle cookies. Before she could even add the first ingredient, a customer had arrived. The entire month of December had been busy, but now that it was only two weeks away from Christmas, it was non-stop. Charlotte's Chocolate Heaven was very popular in both Blue River and the surrounding towns, but word seemed to be spreading even further afield and the chocolate shop was getting busier and busier.

"Be right out." Ally turned off the double-boiler that had begun to melt the chocolate and rushed out into the shop. Already, several customers milled through the shop. Some looked at the assortment of gifts that lined the shelves, including hand-carved wooden toys. Others were fixated on the assortment of chocolate candies in the display counter, while a few more milled about the front counter where silver trays with free samples offered delicious treats.

Ally took a breath and reminded herself that this was only good news, both for Charlotte's Chocolate Heaven, and for the local charity that was collecting donations for the needy. She pushed the donation jar farther out on the counter as she smiled at the customers.

"Please let me know if you have any questions, and don't forget to donate to help those less fortunate. Let's make sure this is a magical holiday for everyone in Blue River and the neighboring towns." Ally smiled and nodded at a woman who dropped a few dollars in the jar. Although things had been crazy, Ally couldn't be happier. With the busy season, her grandmother had been by her side in the shop almost every day that month. Ever since Charlotte Sweet had cut down her hours and handed over the reins of Charlotte's Chocolate Heaven to Ally, she'd been busy with her own activities, and Ally had to admit that she missed not working with her every day.

Ally had grown up in her grandmother's shop and had become accustomed to her being part of her daily life ever since she moved back to Blue River after her divorce. Now, Blue River was home again, and even though many things had changed, one thing remained the same, she never felt more loved than when she smelled the aroma of chocolate and heard the sound of her grandmother humming while she created her confections. There were many times in her life that she'd wanted to get as far away from Blue River as possible, but as an adult, she couldn't think of a single place that she'd rather be. Especially since she had found true love.

"I need totally nut-free candy. Is that even possible?" A short woman with thick glasses and wild, red hair tapped her knuckles lightly against the counter. "Excuse me?"

"Oh, I'm so sorry." Ally smiled at her as she walked over. "Yes, we have a small, separate room where we prepare nut-free candy and then vacuum seal it to be sure there is no cross-contamination. If you'd like I can show you the room and the process."

"No, that's all right, I'll take two boxes please.

And two boxes of your regular assorted candy." She pointed to the small boxes on display, then put her credit card down on the counter.

As Ally rung up the sale, she heard the bell again. This time it signaled her grandmother entering the shop.

She greeted all of the customers with a warm smile and many with a hug. It seemed to Ally that her grandmother knew every single person in Blue River, and many times people who were just passing through. Not many visitors left Blue River without a stop at the chocolate shop.

"Morning Mee-Maw." Ally waved to her as she turned to collect the boxes of candy the customer requested. "We're already going strong."

"I see that." Charlotte laughed and tugged her granddaughter into a tight hug. "'Tis the season." She grinned.

"Yes, it is."

"I see you made it to the shop finally, Lola." Charlotte smiled at the red-headed woman in front of the counter.

"Yes, I can't wait to try these." Lola smiled.

"Lola is from Mainbry, but she works at Nancy's jewelry store." Charlotte looked from Lola to Ally. "This is my granddaughter, Ally."

"Nice to meet you, Lola." Ally smiled brightly.

"You too." Lola nodded.

"Enjoy." Ally handed over the boxes, and a receipt. "Thanks so much, and please come again."

"Oh, don't worry I will." Lola winked at Ally, then hurried out the door. As she stepped out, another surge of customers pushed through the door.

"Oh, Mee-Maw!" Ally rocked back on her heels and took a sharp breath. "This is the busiest I've ever seen the shop."

"Don't worry, we can handle this." Charlotte gave her a light nudge with her elbow.

Ally took a deep breath, then nodded.

"If you want to help the customers, I can get the cookies going in the back."

"Great, because we're almost sold out." Charlotte pointed to the almost empty shelf that a few batches of cookies had taken up just a few minutes before.

"I'm on it." Ally rushed into the back just as the oven timer beeped. She took a batch of cookies out of the oven to cool. Then turned and took the prepared cookie dough out of the refrigerator. Then she turned the double-boiler back on. The cookie dough needed at least three hours in the refrigerator, so she needed to replace the dough to ensure they didn't run out.

As Ally worked on creating a triple batch of cookies, her heart warmed at the thought of how big of a donation they would be able to make. All of their profits from the sale of the special chocolate crinkle cookies would be donated to the local charity, and she could only imagine how much it would help out the struggling families in the area. It had been a tough year for everyone, thanks to tax hikes, job losses, and the cost of everything going up. Ally didn't have to worry too much, as she lived in the cottage that she had grown up in, but she'd felt the pinch in other ways, at the grocery store, and when she had to make shipments from the store. Each time she felt annoyed by it, she thought about how difficult it must be for others under more financial strain to keep up.

Ally placed the newly prepared dough in the refrigerator then started rolling out balls of the cooled dough and dipped them in the sugars. Even though there was so much to do, the repetitive task relaxed her. As soon as she had all the cookies on the baking sheets, she slid them into the oven, set the timer, then started melting more chocolate to make a few batches of candies.

"I cleared them all out, finally." Charlotte poked her head through the kitchen door. "Do you need a break? I can work on the candies and keep an eye on the front."

"No, I'm okay, thanks." Ally glanced over her shoulder at her. "You showed up just in time. What would I do without you?"

"You'll manage. I'm only doing extra hours for the holidays, Ally, remember that." Charlotte grinned. "Jeff and I have big plans to do lots of day trips next year."

"Jeff, huh?" Ally smiled and gave her grandmother a knowing look. "I can't say that I blame you, he is quite the looker."

"Oh Ally!" Charlotte rolled her eyes and laughed. "Speaking of lookers, where is Luke? I thought he was stopping by this morning with some new toys for the donation bin?"

"I'm sure he'll be here soon. There's been an uptick in traffic issues, and domestic disputes, so he's been helping out with patrol to keep up." Ally shook her head. "'Tis the season."

"I wish it wasn't that kind of season." Charlotte scrunched up her nose. "I still can't believe that the jewelry store was robbed. Jeff told me the owner, Nancy, is devastated."

"I'm sure she is." Ally glanced over at her.

"The diamonds that were stolen were a big draw to her shop. Plus, she's still recovering from the robbery itself. How would we feel if this place was robbed?" Charlotte shook her head. "It's not an easy thing to get over."

"That's true, and especially at this time of year, it's quite a rough thing to deal with." Ally looked up as the bell over the door rang out again. "More customers."

"Ally!" A shrill voice sung out from the front of the shop. "Ally! Get out here! It's an emergency!"

"It's Mrs. Bing." Ally rolled her eyes and smiled as she looked over at her grandmother.

"Let's see what kind of emergency she has." Charlotte grinned as she headed out into the main area of the shop.

Mrs. Bing, Mrs. Cale, and Mrs. White, their most loyal and regular customers, crowded around the front counter, and selected candies from the free sample trays.

"This, doesn't look like an emergency." Ally smiled as she leaned against the counter.

"It is though." Mrs. Bing settled her gaze on Ally and pursed her lips. "There are no chocolate crinkle cookies."

"We're working on it." Charlotte laughed as she nodded to each of the women. "It's been a little busy around here."

"No excuse." Mrs. Bing huffed as she popped a candy into her mouth.

"Don't mind her, she's a little cranky." Mrs. White lowered her voice. "They ran out of eggnog at Polly's Place last night, and she hasn't been able to get over that all day."

"Oh, that is disappointing, Polly's Place has the best eggnog." Ally gave Mrs. Bing a light pat on the arm. "I'll get you some cookies." She stepped into the back to retrieve the cookies. She always smiled when she saw the chocolate crinkle cookies, they reminded her of Christmas and snowflakes. With their sugar coated, cracked white surface revealing the delicious chocolate underneath.

When Ally returned, she found the sample tray of candy almost empty. Despite how busy they were, she didn't mind. Mrs. Bing, Mrs. Cale, and Mrs. White were surrogate grandmothers to her, and had been since she was a child.

"Here you go." Ally smiled as she set the plate down in front of them. "I'm so glad you like them. We've been raising quite a bit of money from them."

"I feel like the whole town is caught up in giving

fever." Mrs. White smiled. "It's quite nice to see and to be part of it all."

"Yes, it is." Charlotte tapped the side of the donation jar on the counter. "We've filled quite a few of these. I think this is the first year that I can remember that everything has been so well organized."

"Thanks to Louisa," Mrs. Bing mumbled her words around a large bite of cookie. "Without her, all of it would be a total mess."

"You're absolutely right." Mrs. Cale rolled her eyes. "You should have heard all of the arguing at the community meeting. Everyone had their own ideas of how everything should be done. Then Louisa stood up in the middle of all of the fighting and announced exactly how it was going to be. She said that since she makes the rounds to all the homes and businesses in her mail truck, she would be the one to collect the donation money and deposit it into the account. It made everything so simple. Not only that, but she went around to all of the businesses and got each one to agree to host a jar."

"And they are beautiful jars." Ally gazed at the glass jar that had been painted with poinsettias and stars. "I have a feeling Mrs. White had something to do with that?" She raised an eyebrow as she glanced over at her.

"Maybe." Mrs. White grinned.

The bell rang over the door again and four people walked through the door. She didn't recognize two ladies who looked to be in their twenties, but she did recognize the couple who entered with them. Ally knew the Masons from her grandmother's retirement village, Freely Lakes. Ally greeted them, then the four customers fanned out through the shop.

"I see you're getting busy in here." Mrs. Cale turned towards Mrs. Bing and Mrs. White. "Let's go and let them work, we have our own errands to get to, don't we?"

"Don't remind me." Mrs. Bing groaned. "Lots to do."

As the three ladies left the shop, Ally turned her attention to the new customers. Briefly she caught sight of a face in the front window, one unfamiliar to her. His scraggly curls hung down to just above his eyebrows, pushed down by a knit hat. His eyes carried a haunted look that made her wonder for just a second if he was really there.

"Not again." Charlotte sighed as she walked towards the door. "Ally, I'll take care of this."

"Take care of what?" Ally watched as her grandmother walked out the door, but her attention shifted to the customer in front of her as he asked a question.

By the time she finished with the customers, she'd almost forgotten about her grandmother's words.

Charlotte stepped back inside, with another group of customers. Ally wanted to ask her what she had been up to, but she was swept up in the surge of new customers. A few hours passed before she even had the chance to catch her breath.

"Finally." Charlotte sighed and rubbed her hands together. "Five minutes of peace."

"Five minutes?" Ally looked over at her as she laughed. "I think you're dreaming." The bell over the door punctuated her words. "See?"

"Hi ladies." Louisa Nelson waved as she walked in the door. She had short, brown hair and blue eyes that always seemed to sparkle with warmth. She was followed by two women and a teenage boy. "I see that things are really hopping in here. I'm just here to collect the money from the jar."

"It's a good thing you came when you did." Ally picked up the jar of donations and handed it to her. "It's ready to overflow."

CHRISTMAS COOKIES AND CRIMINALS

"Wow, isn't that just wonderful!" Louisa beamed as she transferred the money from the jar into a zippered pouch. "It's going to be a great holiday for everyone."

"It sure looks like it." Charlotte smiled. "How about you? What are your plans? Any family coming into town?"

"Actually, this Christmas is a very special one for me." Louisa lowered her voice and stepped closer to the counter. "My son has come home to me."

"Oh?" Ally met her eyes. "Tucker?"

"Yes, Tucker." Louisa's eyes filled with tears. "When I heard he was being released just after Thanksgiving, I really thought it was a Christmas miracle. When he came home, he proved that. He's changed so much. He's really turned over a new leaf."

"That's wonderful to hear." Charlotte reached across the counter and rubbed Louisa's shoulder. "No matter how far they wander, they always find their way back. Isn't that right, Ally?" She looked over at her.

"Yes, sure." Ally paused, then raised an eyebrow. "I mean I didn't exactly wander, but I understand what you're saying."

"Sure, sure." Charlotte smiled at her, then patted

her arm. She turned her attention back to Louisa. "So, he's doing well now?"

"Yes. He's learned his lesson. You know he just got caught up with the wrong crowd." Louisa shook her head, then sighed. "Anyway, all that matters is that he is home now, and we can spend Christmas together."

"That is a beautiful thing." Charlotte wrapped her arm around Ally's shoulders. "They have no idea how much we miss them when they are away, do they?"

"Not a clue." Louisa winked at Ally.

"We miss you, too." Ally slung her arm around her grandmother's waist and gave her a solid squeeze. "I'm so glad Tucker is home with you, Louisa. I'll have to come by and say hello sometime."

"I'm sure he'd love to see you. He might actually come and see you about a job. He is just waiting to see if something else comes through first. I hope you don't mind?" Louisa smiled.

"Not at all." Ally grinned. "I remember when he used to come into the chocolate shop with you before I went away to college, he was such a cute kid. He was always laughing."

"It's been hard for him to adjust to being back

home. So many of his old friends have moved out of town, or just won't see him." Louisa frowned as she tucked the zippered pouch into the mailbag that hung at her side. "Not too many people believe in second chances these days. Merry Christmas, ladies. I'll see you tomorrow." She waved to them both before she turned and left the shop.

Ally set the donation jar back down on the counter, as Charlotte walked off to greet the customers.

*a*s Ally looked up from the jar, she caught the eyes of the teenage boy that had walked into the shop. She had seen him around town but had never met him. He looked to be about fifteen or sixteen and had spiky, brown hair and bright blue eyes. At first, she had assumed that he was with the two women, but they didn't speak to or look at him.

"Got any samples?" He smiled at her, revealing dimples.

"Sure, right here." Ally gestured to the sample tray and realized that it was almost empty. "Oops, let me get some more out." She turned around to gather more chocolates for the tray. When she turned back, the boy had the donation jar in his hands. "What are you doing with that?"

Ally narrowed her eyes as the boy shifted the jar from hand to hand.

"Oh, just looking at it." He set it back down and shrugged. "I'm trying to find a gift for my mom."

"Aw, how sweet. I'm afraid that's not for sale, though. We do have an assortment of gift boxes. Does she like chocolate?" Ally looked into the boy's eyes.

"Never mind." He waved his hand, then hurried out through the door.

Ally stared after him for a moment, then turned her attention to ringing up the next customer.

After another flurry of customers, the shop finally began to settle.

"Mee-Maw, you must be ready for a break." Ally smiled at her. "Why don't you head home for the night? I can handle the last few hours, and close up."

"I'll do nothing of the sort." Charlotte pursed her lips. "We're in this together, remember?"

"Yes, we are. Which means, when I see you getting tired, it's my job to insist that you go home." Ally crossed her arms as she looked at her grandmother. "I'll need you more tomorrow, when all of this craziness starts over again."

"Good point." Charlotte stifled a yawn. "Jeff did ask me to meet him for dinner. But maybe we can take a walk first. Some fresh air to wake me up."

"See?" Ally smiled. "You have a good reason to head out. How is Jeff doing?"

"Pretty good. He has branched out into wire-wrapping gemstone jewelry and is really enjoying it." Charlotte pointed to the necklace she wore. "Isn't it gorgeous?"

"Oh, yes it is." Ally eyed it for a moment. "I bet he's pretty busy this time of year with people ordering gifts from him."

"He's doing fairly well." Charlotte nodded. "I was thinking maybe we should have a small display of his jewelry in the shop, just for the Christmas season?"

"I think that's a great idea. There was a boy in here earlier looking for a gift for his mother, I'm sure he would have liked something like that." Ally stretched her arms above her head, then glanced at the clock. "Have a good night, Mee-Maw. Let me know what Jeff says about putting his jewelry on display."

"I will." Charlotte gave her a quick hug, then headed out the door.

Ally released a slow breath. Alone in the shop, she could admit to herself that she was tired. She wasn't alone for long before the bell rang above the door. Ally recognized the woman who stepped inside as the owner of the jewelry store at the end of the street.

"Hi Nancy, how are you?" Ally smiled at her.

"Today was crazy!" Nancy sighed. "I can't complain about the business, but I am worn out! I came in for a few of those cookies everyone is talking about."

"Let me pack some up for you." Ally put together a small bag of cookies and set it on the counter. As she rang up Nancy's purchase for her, she noticed the woman leaned on the counter for support. "Are you doing okay?"

"I think so, I'm just winded. Ever since I turned fifty, it seems like I don't have the energy I used to. Then again, it's been a crazy few weeks." Nancy picked up the bag of cookies. "Thanks so much for these. Back to the grind tomorrow." She waved over her shoulder as she walked out.

Ally took the few moments of quiet to clean up the shop. After sweeping, she aligned the assortment of wooden toys and gifts on the shelves. Her fingertips lingered on the creations as she thought about the amount of work that Luke put into them. She loved to watch him work, though he insisted that it had to be boring for her. Seeing him create something whimsical and new out of what was once just a block of wood, always fascinated her. He had the ability to see beyond the surface, to see potential, and to create something brand new out of what someone else might see as nothing.

Lost in thought, she didn't notice at first when several people hurried past the front window of the shop. It wasn't until she heard a screech of tires, followed by a few shouts, that she looked up through the window and saw a crowd of people gathering in the street. At first, she thought maybe the door-to-door carolers had decided to put on a show in the middle of town, but one look at the tense expressions on the faces of the people in the crowd, indicated that was not the case. She pushed open the door of the shop and stuck her head outside.

"What's all of the commotion about?" Ally looked down the sidewalk in the direction of the crowd of people.

"There's been a robbery." A man walked past her

with a grim expression. She recognized him as Bob from the deli. "All of the donation money was stolen out of the mail truck."

"What?" Ally gasped as she caught sight of the white exterior of the mail truck through the crowd. Several cars had stopped in the middle of the street. A patrol car put on its brakes as it neared the scene. "Louisa wasn't hurt, was she?"

"I don't think so." Bob frowned as he continued past her.

Ally hesitated. Without anyone else in the shop she couldn't leave it unattended, but she wanted to be sure that Louisa was okay. She flipped the sign in the window to closed, then locked the door behind her. As she hurried down the sidewalk, she heard Christmas music playing from one of the nearby stores. Normally, it gave her a cheerful boost, but in that moment, with flashing police lights spilling across the buildings, and a gathering of concerned people, it felt eerie.

"Louisa?" Ally peered through the group of people and saw Louisa huddled close to Luke.

"How could I be so stupid?" Louisa wiped at her eyes as her shoulders trembled. "I was only gone for a few minutes. I just never thought something like this would happen."

"Louisa, don't blame yourself." Luke put his hand on her shoulder.

"Louisa, are you okay?" Ally walked over to her and offered her a tissue.

"I'm so sorry, Ally, everyone is going to be so disappointed in me. I've ruined Christmas!" Louisa took the tissue and wiped at her eyes.

"This isn't your fault. It's the fault of the thief that took the money." Ally opened her arms to her. "I'm so sorry this happened."

"Me too." Louisa hugged Ally, then sighed. "It is my fault. I never should have left the money in the truck. But I got some of that spiced apple cider from Polly's Place, and it went right through me. I stopped just for a minute to use the restroom. I never thought anyone would go into my truck so quick to steal something. I just can't believe it." She blew her nose, then crumpled up the tissue. "I keep thinking of the kids that won't be getting any presents because of me."

"It's not your fault." Ally looked straight into her eyes. "And there's still time to raise more money. We can make it happen."

"Ally, thank you for trying to make me feel better, but I think I just need to get back to work. I still have some mail to deliver on the way home."

Louisa tucked the tissue into her pocket, then turned and walked back towards the truck.

Ally watched her go, her chest tight with frustration. She wished there was something she could do to help her. Even though it wasn't her fault that the money was stolen, she could understand why Louisa felt responsible.

"Luke, any idea who did this?" Ally looked over at him as he jotted something on his notepad.

"Not at the moment." Luke sighed and flicked his gaze around the surrounding buildings. "I'm hoping that there are cameras that caught something." He met her eyes. "I'm sorry I didn't get a chance to bring the toys yet, it's been crazy."

"That's all right." Ally smiled.

"I'd better get back to it." Luke hurried off into the crowd.

As Ally trudged back to the shop, she didn't feel the slightest bit of Christmas spirit. Instead she felt deflated, and frustrated. She noticed a light brown cat with white patches out of the corner of her eye.

"Cinnamon." Ally crouched down and the cat ran over. She patted the cat's back and he purred in response. Cinnamon had been taken in by Carlisle, an elderly gentleman, who lived down the street from the shop. Cinnamon was a beautiful cat and his affection always warmed Ally's heart. Even though a terrible crime had just occurred, the cat brought a smile to her face. She doubted she would see a lot of Cinnamon over the coming days as it was getting much colder. She gave him an extra pat. "See you later, boy." Ally stood up and Cinnamon sauntered down the street towards home, as she headed towards the shop.

CHAPTER 3

*a*lly shivered against the cold breeze that carried down the street as she neared Charlotte's Chocolate Heaven. She couldn't believe that someone would be so heartless and steal the charity money.

"Ally, why is the shop closed?" Charlotte's voice drew her from her thoughts as she walked up to her.

"I went to check on Louisa. I only closed it for a few minutes." Ally frowned as she shoved her hands into her pockets.

"Check on Louisa? Why? Jeff and I were just headed out when we saw all of the commotion. What's happened?" Charlotte looked past her, towards the crowd that had begun to disperse.

"All of the donation money was stolen from

27

Louisa's truck." Ally shook her head as she sighed. "It's terrible. She thinks it's all her fault."

"What? Oh no!" Charlotte winced. "Oh, how terrible for everyone." She waited as Ally opened the door of the shop. "What is going on in this town?"

"I don't know." Ally bit into her bottom lip. "I am definitely not feeling the joy of the season."

"Ally." Charlotte stepped into the shop behind her. "You can't do that, if you lose your cheer, then they win, don't they?"

"Haven't they already?" Ally shoved the keys back into her pocket. "I'm sorry, Mee-Maw, I'm just tired, and frustrated." Tears bit at her eyes as she shook her head. "Whoever took that money must have known that it was there. The thief must have known it was meant to help those in need. Who could be so cruel?"

"There are a lot of desperate people in the world." Charlotte hugged her and stroked her hair. "It's hard to imagine, but there are people who believe they have a right to help themselves to whatever they want, without a thought to the needs of anyone else. I know it's tough to see."

"It is." Ally pulled away from her, then took a deep breath. "Especially at this time of year."

28

"It's been so busy today, you must be tired." Charlotte shook her head. "I'm sorry I took off to see Jeff, I should have stayed to help."

"I wanted you to go. I can handle it." Ally flipped the sign in the window to open. "I do love running the shop, Mee-Maw, all of this just threw me for a loop."

"I understand. Why don't we crank up the music and make some white chocolate coconut stars?" Charlotte smiled. "I know you love making those."

"But we already have a good supply." Ally followed her grandmother into the kitchen. "What about Jeff?"

"Sometimes it's not about what you need on the shelf, it's about what you need in your heart." Charlotte winked at her. "It doesn't hurt to have extra. Jeff and I will have plenty of time together, now I'm going to enjoy some time with you."

Ally spent the rest of the evening creating candies with her grandmother. By the time she closed up, she felt a little better.

When Ally pulled up to her cottage, she immediately felt excited at the thought of seeing her orange cat, Peaches, and her grandmother's pot-bellied pig, Arnold. She walked up the driveway and heard the scratching and meowing from the other side of the cottage door.

"I am so happy to see you two." Ally opened the door and bent down to greet them. Arnold nuzzled her hand and Peaches ran her body against her leg. They always put a smile on her face. "Come, let's go outside." She walked towards the back door as they followed close behind her. The cool air helped her to relax. She watched Arnold chase Peaches for a few minutes, then they ran inside and straight towards the food drawer.

"Hungry?" Ally laughed as she got their bowls and fed them.

After they had finished and Ally had a peanut butter and jelly sandwich, they watched television for a bit. She couldn't keep her eyes open, so they all went to bed. Peaches lay on her stomach and Arnold lay at the foot of her bed. As she stroked Peaches' back, she felt a lot better than she had a few hours before. Yes, a theft had taken place, but at least no one was hurt, and tomorrow would be another day.

Another day that came far too soon. Ally marveled at the sound of her alarm going off.

"But I just closed my eyes," she mumbled groggily as she smacked the button to silence it.

Peaches pounced on top of her and gave a loud meow.

"Yes, yes, I know. Breakfast." Ally pushed herself out of bed and made her way into the kitchen.

As she prepared breakfast for Peaches, Arnold, and herself, she recalled the theft. Again, her thoughts fixated on the idea that it had to be someone who knew that Louisa would be collecting the money. Everyone participating knew, but they certainly wouldn't want to steal the donations. Would they?

Ally quickly latched on Peaches and Arnold's harnesses and took them for a walk. The cool breeze helped clear her head. When she returned home, she took a sip of coffee, then grabbed a muffin on the way out the door. After saying goodbye to Arnold and Peaches, she drove to the shop just in time to open it. Already the streets were busy with holiday shoppers. She tried to feel the excitement she had the day before, but instead her thoughts shifted to all of the people that would not be getting as much help this year. She also thought about what Louisa had been through, and how badly she felt.

The moment she turned the sign to open, customers began to flood the shop. It wasn't until

Mrs. Bing, Mrs. Cale, and Mrs. White walked through the door that she even had the chance to take a breath.

"Morning ladies."

"Morning." Mrs. Cale smiled at her. "We brought you some fresh apple juice." She placed the bottle down on the counter.

"We figured you might not have had time to have a drink, and you need your energy." Mrs. White offered a knowing nod.

"You were right." Ally laughed. "Thank you so much. Please help yourself to some of the samples and let me know if we need more of anything."

"Will do." Mrs. Cale grinned as she picked up one of the candies.

"Have you heard anything from Louisa?" Ally frowned as she took a sip of the juice. "I've been worried about her. She hasn't come into the shop yet today. Maybe she doesn't have any mail for us."

"I've tried to reach her all morning." Mrs. Bing shook her head. "But she hasn't answered. I've tried to catch up with her on her route, but we keep missing each other. Maybe she doesn't want to talk about the theft. I'm sure she is quite upset."

"I would be." Mrs. White crossed her arms. "Just think of the violation you would feel. She never could have expected that someone would break into the mail truck."

"Did Luke say anything about having a suspect?" Mrs. Bing leaned close to Ally.

"Not yet. I actually haven't spoken to him this morning." Ally glanced up as another customer walked into the shop. "Welcome, please let me know if there is anything I can help you with."

"Thanks, I will." He lowered his head and walked the length of the shelves that contained the wooden toys.

"I hope Luke comes up with something soon." Mrs. Bing frowned, then jumped as her cell phone rang. She fished it out of her purse. "Oh, it's Louisa." She smiled as she held up her phone. "I'll put it on speaker so we can all let her know that she has our support." She shot a stern look in Mrs. Cale's direction.

"Yes, yes." Mrs. Cale waved her hand.

"Hi Louisa, we're all here." Mrs. Bing smiled as she held out the phone. "And Ally, too!"

"Hello." Louisa's voice sounded high pitched and rushed. "I've worked out who stole the—" The line cut off.

"Louisa?" Mrs. Bing shouted into the phone. "Are you there? We can't hear you! Louisa?"

"Oh, give me that phone!" Mrs. White rolled her eyes and snatched the phone out of Mrs. Bing's hand. "You probably muted it or something." She tapped the screen a few times. "Louisa? Are you there? Hello?"

Ally held her breath as she watched the three women squabble over the phone. The trio could get very heated at times. As she exhaled, she held her hand out for the phone.

"Does it say call ended?" She skimmed the screen as Mrs. White placed it in her hand. "Yes, it says call ended. It's possible that you just lost signal. Give her a call back." Ally handed the phone back to Mrs. Bing. "It sounded like she might have figured out who stole the donation money."

"Okay, I'll try her." Mrs. Bing dialed the number again. As they listened, the phone rang repeatedly. Then a cheery voice filled the room.

"Merry Christmas! I'm probably busy delivering packages all over town, so please leave me a message and I'll get back to you as soon as I can."

Mrs. Bing frowned as she ended the call.

"I wonder what's going on? Why isn't she answering the phone?"

"It's a busy time of year, sometimes service can get bad around the holidays." Ally frowned, then shrugged. "I'm sure she's fine. Give her a few minutes and she'll call you right back. She is probably just busy."

"Ally's right." Mrs. Cale nodded. "Wouldn't it be exciting if she did figure it out? Maybe we could get the money back in time for Christmas."

"Maybe." Ally smiled at the thought. "I should give Luke a call. Maybe she called him first."

"I just tried her again." Mrs. Bing frowned as she lowered the phone from her ear. "Nothing."

Ally dialed Luke's number as her heartbeat quickened. She was eager to find out what Louisa was going to tell them about the theft. It seemed odd to her that the call would drop and then the phone would ring out. Ever since the new cell phone tower had been erected in town, service had been excellent. But she was probably just reading too much into it. Louisa was probably just busy.

Ally was dying to know who had stolen the money.

"Hi Ally." Luke's warm voice filled her ear.

"Hi Luke." Ally couldn't help but smile. "Have you heard from Louisa? Mrs. Bing just had a strange call from her. I think she figured out who stole the donation money, but before she could tell us the line cut off."

"No, I haven't heard from her." Luke gave a muffled command to someone.

"We tried calling her a few times, but she didn't answer." Ally turned away from the ladies seated at the counter. "I might go check on her later."

"Because of bad cell reception?"

"Luke, you know that the reception is good here. I don't know, I just have a weird feeling. I'm sure it's nothing." Ally glanced over her shoulder. "Mrs. Bing, did she answer this time?"

"No, nothing." Mrs. Bing met Ally's eyes.

"If I hear from her, I'll let you know. If you hear from her, let me know. Okay?" Luke asked.

"Thanks Luke. I'll let you know." Ally ended the call and looked at the others. "Luke hasn't heard anything from her."

A group of customers walked through the door just as the man who had entered previously walked up to the register. Ally spent the next few hours trying to keep up with the demand. When it was time to close up, she felt uneasy as she turned the lock on the door. Mrs. Bing had sent her a text explaining that she still hadn't been able to contact Louisa. The call from Louisa hung in her mind. What if the call hadn't been dropped? What if she was in some kind of trouble? She couldn't imagine what it would be, but she was certain she wouldn't be able to rest without looking into it. She decided to go home first and feed her pets, then if she still hadn't heard from her, she would go check on her.

Ally took one last glance around the shop to be sure everything was in place for the next morning, then stepped out through the side door. She locked the door, then climbed into her car. For a second she relaxed against the seat. That second slid into a minute, and then another. Her body ached from all of the frenzied activity of the day. Her mind swirled with the excitement of the holiday, and the pressure of keeping up with the demand. Then her thoughts settled on Luke. Instantly a smile sprang to her lips. She couldn't wait to have a little uninterrupted time with him. He had said that maybe that evening he could steal away for a few hours.

With all of the petty crimes being committed, he was trying to help the officers keep up, and she knew that he was tired. She planned to give him a good shoulder massage, and then maybe he would give her one, too. She smiled at the thought, then continued on to the cottage she had practically always called home. Her time in the city seemed like a distant memory now. Even the pain of a bad divorce had eased. Once in a while, ghosts of her past spooked her, but in general she'd settled into a happy and satisfying routine in Blue River.

Ally parked in the driveway and spotted a snout in the front window.

"I'm coming, Arnold!" She laughed as she hurried up to the door.

Scratching on the other side indicated that Peaches was ready to get outside for a bit.

"Hi kiddos." Ally grinned as she stepped through the door. "I bet you're hungry. Let's go outside for a bit and then get some dinner." She reached down to pet Peaches as she rubbed along her leg, then scratched behind Arnold's ear. "I missed you both, too."

After taking them outside she got their dinner ready. As Ally set out their dinner, her nerves remained on edge. Louisa remained on her mind.

"I should just put this to rest." She picked up her phone and dialed Luke's number. As the phone rang, she watched Peaches and Arnold devour their food.

"Ally, sorry I don't really have any time to talk." Luke's words were rushed and tense.

"Okay, did you hear from Louisa?" Ally frowned as she realized it didn't look good for their alone time.

"No, I haven't. I presume you haven't either."

"No, but don't worry about it. I know you're busy. I'll go check on her, just to put my mind to rest." Ally smiled.

"Okay, speak to you later." Luke ended the call.

Ally was determined to find out what Louisa had discovered. If she had really figured out who stole the donation money, then maybe the crime could be solved, and the money could go to where it was meant to go.

"I'm going to take a drive over there now and check on her," Ally muttered to herself as she grabbed her keys and purse and started towards the door. As she reached it, her cell phone rang again. She pulled it out of her purse and saw that it was Mrs. Bing calling.

"Hello? Mrs. Bing?"

The line cut off.

Ally's heart dropped. There was no reason to be concerned, she knew that calls could drop, but like the call from Louisa, for some reason this time, it made the hair on the back of her neck stand up.

She called Mrs. Bing's number, but it went straight to voicemail.

Ally frowned as she continued out the door. Maybe speaking to Louisa would help her nerves to settle. Something was certainly going on with the cell service in town, but she doubted it would get straightened out before the holidays were over.

As Ally started the car, her cell phone rang again. This time, it was Luke.

"Hello? Luke? Can you hear me?"

"I can hear you."

"I'm sorry, I think I'm having trouble with my phone." Ally sighed.

"Ally, can you go into the station?" Luke's voice was soft.

"Sure, why?" Ally's heart raced. "Luke, is everything okay?"

"I can't say too much right now, but I know Mrs. Bing would feel better if you were there with her," Luke said quickly. "I have to go, Ally. I'll update you soon."

"Mrs. Bing is at the police station? Luke, what is going on?" Ally frowned as the phone cut off. Had the call dropped, or had he hung up? She had no idea.

As Ally drove towards the police station, she tried to make sense of why Mrs. Bing would be there.

Ally parked, then headed inside. She noticed several officers rushing around with papers, or on their phones. Even the officers manning the front desk barely gave her a wave as she walked past. She spotted Mrs. Bing in Luke's office. The older woman was hunched forward with a tissue pressed against her mouth.

"Mrs. Bing?" Ally stepped inside the office. "What's wrong? Did something happen?"

Mrs. Bing looked up at Ally with wide eyes.

"Louisa's been murdered!"

CHAPTER 4

"*M*urdered?" Ally stared into her eyes as she stepped farther into the office and placed her hand on her friend's shoulder. "Are you sure about that, Mrs. Bing? Or is that some kind of rumor that you've heard?"

"It's no rumor, Ally, I saw her myself." Mrs. Bing clutched the tissue in one hand and rocked forward in her chair as a sob ripped through her. "Oh, I've never seen anything so terrible before. I just wanted to check on her, to make sure that she was okay. So, I went to her house." She looked up at Ally. "The door was open, I just wanted to take a peek inside."

"Oh Mrs. Bing, I'm so sorry." Ally pulled a chair over next to Mrs. Bing's and sat down beside her.

Her heart pounded as she wondered if somehow Mrs. Bing could be mistaken. "Tell me everything that happened, from the beginning."

"I called out for her, but she didn't answer me. I knew that she wouldn't just leave her door open like that, so I went inside to have a look. I thought maybe I would find Tucker and his buddies hanging out in the kitchen or something. You know how kids are." Mrs. Bing rolled her eyes, then sighed. "But it wasn't Tucker. It was only Louisa. She was on the couch, I thought she was fine at first, but when I tried to speak to her, she didn't answer. Then I realized that she was gone." Mrs. Bing shook her head as she looked up at Ally. "I think she was strangled, but I'm not sure."

"That's terrible, Mrs. Bing." Ally hugged her, then looked into her eyes. "I'm so sorry that you had to go through this."

"Sorry for me?" Mrs. Bing narrowed her eyes. "Absolutely not, I'll not have that." She straightened up in her chair. "Don't waste a second of your time doting over me, what we need to focus on is what happened to Louisa."

"I'm sure that Luke is already working hard on the investigation." Ally glanced over her shoulder at the office door as she wondered where he might be. "Don't worry, he will get to the bottom of all of it."

"He's at Louisa's house still. One of the officers wouldn't stop asking me questions, it was very upsetting, so he insisted that I get taken back here out of the cold." Mrs. Bing shivered, then sighed. "Not that I feel any warmer. I just can't believe this happened. Who would do this terrible thing to her?"

"I'm not sure. But we will find out." Ally patted her hand gently and met her eyes. "Just try to let yourself rest, you've been through a lot."

"I can't." Mrs. Bing shook her head. "Ally, we can't just leave this to the police. They have rules they have to follow. We need to look into this ourselves. Will you help me?"

"Of course, I will." Ally leaned closer to her and lowered her voice. "But you have to understand, Mrs. Bing, we're not talking about investigating a new neighbor here, we're talking about finding a murderer."

"I do understand. I found Louisa, remember? I know exactly what happened to her." Mrs. Bing shivered again, then curled her hand around Ally's. "That's all the more reason to look into it. It can't hurt right? Luke will do things his way, and we will do things our way."

"I'm sure he wouldn't mind the help." Ally's heart pounded at the thought. She was actually quite certain of the opposite. He would warn her against interfering with the investigation, he would point out the risk to Mrs. Bing, and he would mention the fact that his training, badge and gun afforded him more protection than the average citizen. But none of that would convince her not to do it. She also knew that Mrs. Bing was one of the most stubborn people she had ever met. She wouldn't stop until she had her answers, and she couldn't let her stumble headlong into something that might end up getting her hurt, or worse. "But you have to promise me one thing, Mrs. Bing."

"What's that?" Mrs. Bing squeezed Ally's hand.

"We do this together." Ally looked into her eyes. "That means no running off and looking into things yourself. Okay?"

"Okay, I promise." Mrs. Bing smiled, then released her hand and patted her cheek. "Ally, I knew I could count on you. So, where do we start?"

"We start with you getting some rest tonight." Ally started to stand up from the chair.

"Ally, no!" Mrs. Bing tugged her back down. "I can't rest. I can't even close my eyes without seeing poor Louisa in my mind. We can't put things off until tomorrow. We have to start tonight, while things are still fresh in my mind. That's what all of the television shows say, right?"

"Right." Ally took a deep breath, then nodded. "Why don't you start with telling me about the moment you arrived at Louisa's house?"

"But I've already told you all of that." Mrs. Bing frowned. "I found her dead on the couch."

"No, I want to know about before that. When you arrived at the house. Did you see anyone nearby? Were there any cars on the street? Was there anyone walking down the sidewalk?" Ally narrowed her eyes. "If the killer was still nearby you might have even seen him or her."

"It's possible. I did see a red truck. It was parked in Louisa's street and it started up when I was pulling into Louisa's driveway. I noticed it because it was such a bright red color." Mrs. Bing shrugged. "But I only glanced at it."

"Was it still there when you came out of the house? Parked nearby?" Ally pulled out her phone to make a note about the red truck.

"I don't think so." Mrs. Bing shivered, then took a deep breath. "When I was in the house, after I found Louisa, I had the strangest feeling, as if someone else was there. I'm sure it was just paranoia."

"Was it just a feeling, or did you hear or notice something that made you think someone else was there?" Ally's fingertips hovered over her phone as she looked at Mrs. Bing.

"I can't remember." Mrs. Bing sighed, then pressed her hand against her forehead.

"It's okay, Mrs. Bing. Don't put too much pressure on yourself." Ally patted her knee, then stood up from her chair. "Why don't we get you home?"

"Wait." Mrs. Bing looked up at her, her eyes wide. "I did hear something."

"What was it?" Ally moved closer to her.

"A thump. No, not exactly a thump." Mrs. Bing pursed her lips as she considered it. "It sounded like a door, opening or closing. That's why I thought someone else was there. But I wasn't sure that I'd even heard it. I was so shocked by what I saw, I wasn't thinking straight."

"I'm sure." Ally made a quick note on her phone. "Did you tell Luke that someone else might have been there?"

"I don't think I mentioned it, no." Mrs. Bing

frowned. "I answered a lot of questions, though. I might have said something about it."

"Well, we obviously know someone else was in the house at some point." Ally sighed as she sat back in her chair. Then she raised an eyebrow. "What about her phone, Mrs. Bing? Did you see Louisa's phone anywhere?"

"Actually, no I didn't. But I didn't exactly look around too much. I guess I should have." Mrs. Bing spread her hands out in front of her. "How are we going to figure this out, when I didn't even pay attention?"

"Mrs. Bing, you didn't know you needed to pay attention. You were in shock. You probably still are." Ally helped her to her feet. "Let me take you home where you will be more comfortable."

"I'm not sure that I'll ever feel comfortable again." Mrs. Bing clutched Ally's arm tightly as she followed her through the door.

Ally felt for the woman who was usually so boisterous and determined to be cheerful. In that moment she knew with certainty that she would do absolutely anything to help solve this crime, so that justice would be served, and Mrs. Bing could find some closure and move on from this.

CHAPTER 5

After Ally left Mrs. Bing's house, she headed back to her cottage. She stepped inside to the sounds of little feet headed straight for her. Despite the events of the day she couldn't help but smile at Peaches and Arnold. Peaches weaved through her legs as she walked towards the couch. Arnold bumped her hand with his soft snout.

Ally sank down on the couch and closed her eyes. Peaches and Arnold jumped right up onto the couch beside her. Arnold settled his head on her leg, and Peaches rubbed her cheek along Ally's.

"I'm sorry, sweet ones. I'm a little distracted." Ally ran her hands along Peaches' soft fur, and Arnold's smooth skin. Cuddles with her two favorite animals made anything weighing on her mind seem far lighter. But at that moment all she could think of was Mrs. Bing, and Louisa.

A sharp knock on the door startled her.

Before she could even open her mouth or stand up, the door swung open, and her grandmother burst in, followed by her friend Jeff.

"Ally! I just heard." Charlotte reached down to greet Arnold as he jumped down from the couch and ran over to nuzzle her.

Peaches curled up in Ally's lap and flicked her tail a few times as she eyed the others. She could be very protective of Ally, especially when she could tell something was troubling her.

"Mee-Maw, I can't believe she's gone." Ally looked up at her.

"Neither can I." Charlotte sat down beside her on the couch. Arnold hopped right up beside her, snuggled close, and set his head on her leg. "Jeff and I had just finished dinner when Luke called me, he asked me to check in with you, and he explained that you were with Mrs. Bing."

"Mee-Maw, she's so upset. I've never seen her like this." Ally wiped at her eyes.

"No one expected this, I think we are all in shock." Charlotte took her hand and rubbed it between her own. "How are you holding up?"

"I'm okay." Ally sighed. "I've been so focused on Mrs. Bing, but honestly, I feel a little guilty for not going straight away to check on Louisa myself."

"None of us could have imagined what happened to her." Jeff took a seat on the other couch.

"Mrs. Bing did." Ally took a slow breath. "Or at least, she wanted to be sure that she was okay. I was about to go check on her. If no one went to check on her it might not have been until tomorrow that anyone noticed." Her eyes widened. "Her son, Tucker, he was living with her right? Has anyone contacted him?"

"I'm not sure." Charlotte frowned as she pulled out her phone. "But the news is certainly getting around town."

"Luke would have tried to contact him." Ally relaxed against the couch and ran her hand along Peaches' fur. "I'm sure he will do his best to track him down." She sighed as she looked up at her grandmother. "Mrs. Bing asked me to help her investigate the crime."

"What?" Charlotte's eyes widened.

"She doesn't want to just leave it to the police. I promised her I'd look into things a bit and try to help find the murderer. I think she just needs to do something." Ally stroked Peaches' ears. "It can't hurt, right?"

"Just take it one step at a time." Jeff leaned forward and tried to meet her eyes. "Listen Ally, what happened to Louisa is terrible, but it is not your job to figure it out. You have a lot on your plate already. You should leave this to the police. You shouldn't let this get under your skin."

"It's impossible not to. Mrs. Bing will look into this either way and I want to help her." Ally frowned and looked down at Peaches, who looked up at her with narrowed eyes. "There's a murderer loose in Blue River, and until we know exactly what happened, it's going to be on all of our minds. Louisa." She sighed. "She didn't deserve this. She worked so hard to raise money for the community, and it got her killed."

"Is that what you think?" Charlotte raised an eyebrow. "That whoever stole the money killed her?"

"Remember Louisa's phone call to Mrs. Bing?" Ally looked up at her. "She said that she had figured out who stole the money. Maybe she confronted the person. Maybe the thief found out she knew and wanted to get rid of her."

"Or maybe the thief was living under her roof." Jeff spoke in a soft tone, but his words were firm.

"Maybe." Ally took a sharp breath. "But I don't think so. I just can't, or don't want to believe that Tucker would kill his mother."

"It's possible." Charlotte cleared her throat. "If she found out that he stole the money, he might have panicked. He might have been so afraid of going back to prison, that he killed her."

"Of course, it's possible. But it's terrible to consider." Ally shook her head. "He was such a cute kid. Louisa and Tucker used to come into the shop. They adored each other."

"They did. But Tucker changed. He isn't a kid anymore." Charlotte patted her hand. "You should take a breath. Just relax."

"I can't." Ally sighed. "I need to do something to help Mrs. Bing and what will help her is finding out the truth. Or at least trying to find out the truth. It won't bring Louisa back, but at least it's something, and it's all I can offer Mrs. Bing. I want to help her through this."

"Okay, I understand." Charlotte nodded. She knew all too well where Ally had gotten her curious and stubborn nature.

"I'll call Luke and see if I can get any

information about where Tucker is, any leads he might have that he'll share. If he is too busy, he won't answer." Ally pulled her phone out of her purse and called Luke.

Luke answered on the fourth ring.

"Hi sweetheart."

"Hi." Ally smiled at the sound of his voice.

"How is Mrs. Bing?"

"I got her settled at home. She's doing the best she can." Ally took a quick breath. "Have you contacted Tucker?"

"Actually, I have him at the station."

"What?" Ally's heart began to race. "Do you have proof that he did this?"

"No, right now he's just a person of interest. But there is good reason to suspect him." Luke paused, exchanged a few words with someone, then spoke to Ally again. "Things are pretty busy here right now. Are you doing okay?"

"Yes." Ally frowned. "Did you figure out a time of death, yet?"

"Not just yet, but it does look like it had been a few hours before Louisa was discovered." Luke lowered his voice. "Ally, you need to leave this to me."

"I am, I'm just curious." Ally shrugged.

"I'm sorry, Ally, I have to go." Luke ended the call.

Ally sighed and looked down at her phone. When she looked up at her grandmother again, she could see the concern in her eyes.

"Luke has Tucker in custody." Ally shook her head. "I want to go down there and talk to him."

"Do you think that's a good idea?" Jeff asked.

"I can't just sit around. I have to do something." Ally shook her head. "I want to talk to Tucker."

"All right, all right. There's no rush." Charlotte looked into her eyes. "If that's what you want to do, you know that I will be by your side every step of the way. Whatever it takes to get this settled, I am here to help. If Tucker is innocent, I can't think of a better way to honor Louisa, than to help find out who the murderer is, and make sure that her son isn't sent back to prison."

"Me too." Jeff looked between them both. "I'm not sure what I can do, but anything I can do, I will do."

Ally picked up Peaches, gave her a kiss on the top of the head, then set her down on the couch as she stood up.

"We're going to have to find out where Tucker was every minute of the day today. The sooner we can find out what he was up to, the sooner we can know if he is a viable suspect."

"This can all be done tomorrow." Jeff frowned.

Ally shook her head.

"No, I don't want to wait until tomorrow." Ally reached for her purse. "I'm going to go down there and see if I can speak to Tucker."

"Just take a breath, Ally." Charlotte scooted Arnold out of her lap then stood. "Jeff's right, you need to think before you run into things. I know you want to do something to help, but you need to try to relax."

"How can I relax when a killer is out there roaming the streets?" Ally looked into her grandmother's eyes.

"We don't know that." Jeff shook his head. "Just take a breath. Right now, all we know is that Louisa has been killed."

"Right, which means there's a killer out there?" Ally shrugged. "I want to do something. I don't want to just sit here."

"I just think you need to slow down a little." Jeff frowned as he sat back against the couch. "Tucker is already in custody."

"I know, but what if he's innocent." Ally took a sharp breath.

"He might be, but he might be guilty." Jeff met her eyes. "You have to consider the fact that he had access to the home, and a possible motive to kill her. He would have known about the money she was collecting, too."

"I know it's easy to assume he was involved because he's just been released from prison." Ally sighed. "But I just don't think he could have done this, and I promised Mrs. Bing that I would help her do a little investigating. It's better to do something than to just sit around thinking about it."

"But Mrs. Bing would want to know what is happening. You should let her know before you see Tucker. And Mrs. Bing needs her rest, too." Charlotte frowned. "She's probably sleeping already."

"You're right." Ally sank back down on the couch. "I shouldn't bother her right now."

A light knock on the door sounded, before the door swung open.

Arnold rushed forward to greet the person at the door.

"Oh, do calm down, Arnold, do behave." Mrs. Bing huffed as she shooed the pig away from her skirt.

"He's so excited to see you." Charlotte stood up and guided Arnold away from Mrs. Bing.

"He's such a sweetheart." Mrs. Bing gave him a light pat, then looked up at Ally. "I know you wanted me to stay home and rest, but I just couldn't. Charlotte, I'm glad that you're here, too. We need to get down to business." She nodded to Jeff and offered a quick smile.

"How are you doing?" Ally stood up to hug her.

"I'll be better when people stop asking me that." Mrs. Bing rolled her eyes. "My phone has not stopped ringing, I guess the news is getting around."

"I'll get some tea on." Charlotte headed for the kitchen and gestured for Jeff to follow her.

Peaches prowled along the back of the now empty couch. She eyed the feathers that stuck out of the side of Mrs. Bing's hat.

"Did you find anything out?" Mrs. Bing met Ally's eyes.

"Only that Luke has Tucker in custody." Ally shook her head. "But I wanted to ask you about the exact time that you spoke to Louisa today. When the call dropped."

"I spoke to Luke already and gave him the information. It was just after eleven. Two minutes after eleven." Mrs. Bing bit into her bottom lip.

"When I think about that being the last time I spoke to her, I just can't believe it."

"Me too." Ally frowned. "I was hoping that maybe you could tell me what you know about Tucker."

"Is it true that he did it?" Mrs. Bing took a sharp breath. "What a terrible thing to imagine."

"We don't know for sure, yet. I can understand why he's a suspect, but I just don't want to believe it." Ally frowned as she reached down to give Arnold a pat. "I don't know him well, but he was a cute kid. He always used to come into the chocolate shop, and he seemed to adore his mother. She adored him, too. And for a son to do something like that to his mother, it's so extreme."

"It wouldn't surprise me if he had." Mrs. Bing pursed her lips. "Apparently, since he's grown up, he's become so ungrateful."

"What do you mean?" Ally guided her towards the couch.

"You know that Louisa was a single mother. She worked day and night to take care of that boy. But as soon as he hit his teens, he was always getting himself into trouble. None of us were surprised when he landed up behind bars." Mrs. Bing rolled her eyes. "Some kids, there's just no hope for them."

"That's a little harsh, don't you think?" Ally sank down onto the couch beside her.

"Not harsh enough if it turns out that he is the one who did this to his mother." Mrs. Bing balled her hands into fists. "Poor Louisa."

"Did you see Tucker much since he's been back in town?" Ally asked.

"A few times. I know that he was out looking for a job. He applied at a few places, but most places won't hire you with a record." Mrs. Bing clucked her tongue. "I overheard Louisa trying to get him a job at the diner."

"Louisa mentioned that he might come and look for a job with us, she was just waiting to see if something else came through." Ally raised an eyebrow. "I know he didn't have a job yesterday. But do you know if he found anyone to hire him since?"

"Louisa said that Jen at the library was going to see what she could do. She seemed to be pretty relieved, so I'm guessing that Jen had assured her it would work out. But I don't know if anything ever came of it." Mrs. Bing accepted a cup of tea from Charlotte. "Thank you so much."

"And for you, Ally." Charlotte offered her a cup.

"Thanks." Ally took the hot cup and held it

between her palms. The warmth helped her to relax. "That might be a good place to start then. If he did start working at the library, Jen might be able to tell us where he was today."

"But the library is closed." Charlotte gave her a knowing look. "And I think we all need some rest."

"Okay, we'll have to leave it until tomorrow. I might try see Tucker in the morning. I think it's best if I go by myself. He might be more forthcoming with information if there's only one of us there. Is that okay, Mrs. Bing?" Ally sat forward.

"Yes, but you must keep me updated." Mrs. Bing narrowed her eyes slightly.

"Of course." Ally smiled.

"Oh my, what's happening?" Mrs. Bing gasped and reached up for her hat as it flew off the top of her head.

Peaches gave a yowl as she pulled the hat onto the back of the couch and pounced on the feathers.

"Peaches!" Ally shouted, then laughed. As the laughter burst past her lips, she tried to wrestle the hat from the cat.

"Bad kitty!" Mrs. Bing fluffed her thin, silver curls, which had been pushed down by the hat. "That's my hat!"

Ally laughed even harder as she finally freed the hat from Peaches and handed it over to Mrs. Bing.

"I'm so sorry. If she did any damage, I'll pay to replace it."

"It's fine, I'm sure." Mrs. Bing fluffed the feathers, then placed the hat back on the top of her head. "It's probably best if we call it a night." She turned and headed for the front door.

Ally covered her mouth as a few giggles slipped past.

"Leave it to Peaches to make you laugh." Charlotte hugged her. "I'll catch up with you in the morning."

"Okay." Ally smiled as she walked her grandmother and Jeff to the door. "Thank you, Mee-Maw."

Ally waved to them both as they walked down the driveway to Jeff's car. She watched until they drove away, then she closed the door.

Ally turned back towards the living room just in time to see Peaches prowl across the back of the couch with a bit of feather hanging from her mouth.

CHAPTER 6

*A*lly's eyes opened the next morning, with a tail in her face and a snout against her back. She smiled at the comfort of her precious pets.

"Morning, guys." She stroked both of their backs. Then she remembered the events of the previous day. If someone had just gone over to check on Louisa after the call dropped, maybe her life could have been saved. Or did the call cut off because Louisa was about to be murdered? There was so much to work out and to do. She showered and dressed. When she stepped out of her bedroom she was greeted by the delicious smell of coffee.

"Mee-Maw?"

"Hi sweetheart, I just wanted to make sure you had a decent breakfast." Charlotte handed her a cup of coffee and pointed to the table where a few pancakes were stacked on a plate.

"You didn't have to do all of this." Ally smiled as she met her grandmother's eyes.

"I didn't, but I wanted to. I wanted to see if you had any thoughts about what happened to Louisa. Jeff." Charlotte called towards the front door that had just swung open. "Pancakes are ready!" She turned back to Ally. "He took Arnold and Peaches out for a walk, so they'll be all set for a few hours."

Ally held back a giggle as she watched Arnold prance through the door in a thick pink sweater, followed by Peaches in her harness.

"It's cold out there?" Charlotte pursed her lips.

"Yes, it is." Jeff shivered as he closed the door behind him. "I am a bit jealous of Arnold's sweater."

"Don't worry, I'm working on yours." Charlotte winked at him.

"Wonderful." Jeff grinned at her.

"Peaches refused to let me put a sweater on her. But she was eager to wear her harness." Charlotte laughed. "She loves exploring."

Ally sat down at the table and gazed down at the pancakes. She didn't want to hurt her grandmother's feelings, but she wasn't very hungry.

"Ally, you have to eat something." Charlotte sat down across from her.

Ally cut off a small piece of pancake and placed it in her mouth. As soon as the first taste hit her taste buds, she became ravenous. Within seconds all of the pancakes were gone.

"Thanks, it's delicious." Ally finished her coffee, then stood up from the table. "We need to figure out how Tucker fits into all of this. If he was just released from prison, then he is probably on parole." She began to pace back and forth through the living room. "If we can reach his parole officer, we might be able to find out more information about him."

"I don't think they just hand out that kind of information." Jeff frowned as he watched her pace. "I mean, they're not going to give you details."

"Unless!" Ally held up one finger and stopped pacing. "Unless we tell the parole officer that we are calling about him because we are thinking about offering him a job. We can pretend like we don't know anything about Louisa. Then the parole officer might give us more information, or at least something that we can go on with. It's worth a try, right?"

"It certainly is." Charlotte nodded as she sat down beside Jeff. "Since he grew up around here, we can look into whether he still has any local connections that might give us some guidance as to what he was up to recently. And, we need to speak with Jen at the library."

"All very good ideas." Jeff glanced over at Charlotte. "But what about the shop? Doesn't it need to be opened up early?"

"Oh, yes it does." Ally blinked, she'd almost forgotten about the holiday season and all of the orders that would be coming in that she was already going to be behind on. "I'd better get there and fast."

"Ally, I can take over today if you'd like." Charlotte stood up. "I doubt you got much sleep last night, thinking about all of this."

"I slept, not well, but that doesn't mean that I can't still work. Besides, I may overhear something that could lead us to good information. I'll go into the shop and make the call to the parole officer from there, it will look more legitimate that way. Maybe you and Jeff could make the rounds locally to see if anyone is in contact with Tucker?" Ally raised an eyebrow as she looked between them.

"I think you'd have better luck with the young people." Jeff cleared his throat. "I'm sure that they would respond to you better."

"Maybe, but they also might say less to me. Tucker is younger than me, we weren't in the same class, and most of the kids I went to high school with have moved away from Blue River." Ally shrugged. "I think you'd have just as much luck. You should start with Ashley at Polly's Place. From memory I think they were friends growing up."

"Okay, we'll give it a try." Charlotte gave Jeff a light slap on the knee. "Let's go mingle with the youth."

"Oh boy, I'd better change my shirt." Jeff snapped the collar of his Hawaiian shirt. "Or is this back in style now?" He laughed.

"You look great." Charlotte took his hand and led him out the door. "I'll check on Peaches and Arnold around lunchtime, Ally, and if you want me to come in and help, or take over anytime this morning, just call me, okay?"

"I will." Ally walked with them to the door. "Just be careful. If Tucker didn't do this, then we have no idea who the killer might actually be. I don't want anyone getting hurt."

"Don't worry, we'll be fine." Jeff met her eyes then draped his arm around Charlotte's shoulders.

Ally watched them go, then turned back to find Peaches perched on the back of the couch.

"Hey sweetheart." Ally walked over to the cat and stroked her fur. "How are you this morning?"

Peaches meowed.

"I know, there's a lot going on." Ally scooped the cat up into her arms. "I've been trying to work this all out in my head, but I just don't have enough to go on." She carried her into the kitchen and prepared her breakfast. As she set the bowl down on the floor, Peaches jumped out of her arms and landed on the floor. She laughed.

Ally put some extra food in Arnold's bowl, then headed out the door. When she arrived at the chocolate shop, she hurried through the morning opening routine, then grabbed the phone. It took a few phone calls, but she was finally able to connect with the correct department, and the parole officer assigned to Tucker.

"I'm calling because I've received an application from Tucker Nelson to work at my shop. I'm considering hiring him, but I'd like to know a little bit more about him first."

"I'm afraid I can't share too much information. What would you like to know?" The voice on the other end of the phone sounded strained.

"Is he in good standing with you? Has he been meeting all the requirements of his parole? I don't want to hire him only to have him get taken back to prison. That would really leave me in the lurch." Ally struggled to stock the display window with candy while keeping the phone cradled between her ear and shoulder.

"He seems like a nice kid. However, at this time I can't provide a reference." He cleared his throat. "Hopefully, I should be able to provide something in the next few days."

Ally's eyes narrowed. It wasn't the response she had expected.

"And why is that?" She set the tray of candies down and pressed the phone against her ear.

"I can't say more than that at this time, I'm sorry. Send me through your details and I will provide a reference when and if I can."

"Thanks for your time." Ally frowned as she hung up the phone. She guessed that if the parole officer couldn't provide a reference for Tucker at this time, then he may have violated his parole. That didn't bode well for his innocence.

CHAPTER 7

*C*harlotte stepped into Polly's Place and tried not to be overwhelmed by the flashing lights. The décor in the restaurant landed somewhere between glitter and strobe lighting. She wondered who had come up with the decorative ideas.

"Wow, I might need my sunglasses." Jeff chuckled as he guided her farther into the restaurant. "Have you ever been in here during the holidays before?"

"Not this year." Charlotte frowned as she straightened the collar of her blouse. "It's not usually like this. I'm not sure what the goal is here, but if it's to give their customers a headache, then it's been met. I know Polly has eccentric tastes and

Ashley, her daughter, has been trying to modernize the place for her, but I don't know what to call this."

"Just try to focus on the counter, it's less flashy there." Jeff winked at her, then steered her towards the front counter.

"Hi Charlotte, Jeff." Ashley, the young woman behind the counter smiled at them. "What can I get for you?"

"I'll just have a coffee, black." Charlotte smiled in return. "And I wanted to talk to you about Tucker Nelson?"

"Tucker?" Ashley nodded as she glanced at Jeff. "And for you?"

"Do you have hot cocoa?" Jeff looked up at the menu on the wall behind her.

"Mint, cinnamon, raspberry, pumpkin spice, apple caramel, apple cinnamon, or apple pie?" Ashley met his eyes.

"Uh. Hot cocoa?" Jeff raised an eyebrow.

"I guess we have that." Ashley glanced over her shoulder. "Sure, I can make you some without adding the flavoring."

"Great." Jeff chuckled.

"I understand you and Tucker went to high school together, right?" Charlotte followed her as the young woman walked from the counter to the coffee pots.

"Yes. Do you know Tucker?" Ashley poured coffee into a cup, then handed it over to Charlotte.

"Just from when he was growing up." Charlotte tipped her head towards the door. "He used to come into the chocolate shop with his mother quite a bit. He might want to work at the chocolate shop and I just thought I'd chat with a few of his friends to see if it's a good idea."

"Well, we aren't really friends anymore." Ashley poured the hot cocoa, then handed the cup to Jeff.

"Did you lose touch after high school?" Jeff took the cup and smiled at her. "It smells delicious."

"Good." Ashley walked over to the register. "No, we kept in touch after high school, I even went to visit him while he was in prison. But since he's been out, he's been avoiding my calls. I can tell you that he'd be a great employee based on what I used to know about him. But I don't know what's going on with him since he's been out."

"I wonder why he would be avoiding your calls?" Charlotte frowned as she handed over some cash to pay for the drinks. "Have you noticed anything odd about him?"

"I ran into him one day last week. I thought I'd

finally have the chance to talk to him, since he couldn't just ignore my call. But when I tried to talk to him, he just walked away. He said I needed to stay away from him." Ashley frowned. "It was rude. It's not like I was stalking him or anything."

"Maybe he thinks you have a romantic interest in him?" Jeff coughed. "Or what do they call it now? You want to hook up?"

"Uh." Ashley gazed at Jeff for a moment then shook her head. "No, things were never like that between us. I was really angry with him at first, but the more I thought about it, the more it seemed odd instead of rude. He walked away from me so fast, almost as if he was afraid to be seen with me." She tilted her head to the side. "I can't say for sure that he wasn't just trying to get away from me. But something about it, felt a little different." She frowned as she met Charlotte's eyes. "I couldn't shake the feeling that maybe he'd gotten himself into something he shouldn't have."

"Maybe your instincts were right." Charlotte took her change, then tossed the coins into the tip jar. "What about his mother? Did he ever mention anything to you about her?"

"Oh, his mother?" Ashley's eyes widened. "That was a very sore subject for him."

"Why is that?" Jeff stepped up beside Charlotte.

"Oh, you don't know?" Ashley looked between the two of them. "She's the one that turned him in to the police. She's the reason that he went to prison in the first place."

"What?" Charlotte gasped. "Are you sure about that?"

"Yes. He was hiding out in the basement, and she reported to the police where he was and where the stolen goods could be found." Ashley chewed on her bottom lip. "I tried to convince him that it was because she wanted him to get help, but Tucker was pretty angry about it. I was surprised when I found out he was living with her."

"Maybe they reconciled when he was released." Charlotte looked over at Jeff.

"Maybe." Jeff frowned.

"All I know is, he's not the same person anymore." Ashley crossed her arms as she looked out through the front window of the shop. "I don't know what happened, and honestly at this point, I don't want to know anymore."

"Thanks for the information." Jeff folded a few dollars into the tip jar, then held the door open for Charlotte.

"If you do hear from him, Ashley, please let me

know." Charlotte handed her a business card with the shop's phone number on it. "If he's in some kind of trouble, I'd like to help."

"Sure, maybe you'll have better luck." Ashley tucked the business card into her pocket, then turned to greet another customer.

"What do you think?" Jeff murmured in Charlotte's ear as he let the door fall closed behind them.

"I think Tucker was hiding things." Charlotte winced as she wrapped her hand around Jeff's. "I know that Ally doesn't think that he had anything to do with his mother's murder, but it sounds to me like he might have been holding onto a grudge."

"Ashley did mention that he was acting scared, too, though." Jeff squeezed her hand as they walked across the street towards the chocolate shop. "Maybe whoever he was scared of, was after him, but came across his mother instead?"

"I'm not sure which would be worse." Charlotte sighed. "I'd hate to discover that something he did led to his mother's death."

Jeff pulled open the door to the chocolate shop just in time to see Ally sell a stack of boxes of candy to a customer.

"Thanks, I promise I'll have the rest of your

order ready by this evening." Ally flashed Charlotte a smile as Jeff held the door for the customer. "I hope you found out more information than I did."

"Actually, we found out a few things." Charlotte relayed the information Ashley had given her. "I do think we have to consider that it's possible Tucker might have done this."

"His parole officer didn't make things look any better." Ally sighed as she shared the information she'd been given. "You know what all of this means, don't you?"

"Maybe Tucker really did this?" Charlotte braced herself. She knew that once Ally had decided on something it was difficult to change her mind.

"Maybe, but it also means that Tucker is in danger of being convicted of a crime that he might not have committed." Ally pursed her lips.

"Ally, why are you so sure?" Jeff met her eyes.

"Honestly, I'm not sure." Ally pulled off her apron. "But I'm going to try to find out one way or the other. I want to talk to Tucker, face to face. I don't want to wait any longer. Mee-Maw, can you handle the shop for an hour or two?"

"Absolutely." Charlotte took the apron from her. "Do you think Luke will let you talk to him?"

"I hope so." Ally grabbed her purse and keys.

"Maybe you should go with her, Jeff." Charlotte frowned as she watched Ally race for the door.

"No thanks." Ally waved over her shoulder.

"I'm staying right here." Jeff stepped behind the counter and grabbed one of the aprons that hung behind it. "Trust me, you're going to need my help." His eyes widened as he watched a crowd of people head straight through the door.

CHAPTER 8

*a*lly looked into Luke's eyes as he held up his hands and frowned.

"It's not common practice to let a civilian speak to a suspect."

"I'm just a visitor." Ally shrugged. "He's allowed visitors, isn't he?"

"Ally, at this point he's likely going to go from being detained for questioning, to being arrested." Luke stepped closer to her. "He lied to us about his alibi. He claimed that he was at a meeting with his parole officer, and then stayed in the area for several hours. That would have cleared him, since according to the medical examiner it's looking like the time of death was between eleven and one. It hasn't been confirmed yet, but that is the best estimate we have so far. It should have been simple to rule Tucker out, but his parole officer never saw him and was about to report him for a parole violation. I know you think he's probably innocent of all of this, but it's not looking that way."

"He lied?" Ally frowned. "That doesn't look good."

"No, it doesn't." Luke placed his hand on her shoulder and looked into her eyes. "Maybe you should let this go. I know you're swamped with the shop."

"I can't, Luke. I'm sorry. Can't I talk to him just for a few minutes?" Ally looked towards the holding cells. "He hasn't been charged with anything yet, right?"

"Not at the moment." Luke leaned back against the wall and closed his eyes. "I'm waiting for the arrest warrant to come through."

"I just want to see him, Luke. I won't cause any trouble." Ally settled her hands on his shoulders and looked into his eyes.

"Ally, I'll let you see him, but you need to understand something." Luke straightened up and placed his hands on top of hers. "He missed his meeting with his parole officer. He doesn't have any good explanation for that. He could have been arrested just for that. So why would he risk missing his appointment if he knew what the consequences would be?"

"Did he say where he was? Why he didn't make it?" Ally frowned.

"No, he is refusing to answer our questions. He won't say where he was." Luke quirked an eyebrow as he met her eyes. "If you knew what was at risk, would you miss your parole appointment without a very good reason?"

"So, you think he's hiding something?" Ally's eyes widened at the thought. Her heart sank. She could only think of one reason why he might hide the truth, and she guessed Luke thought of the same reason. Had Tucker killed his own mother?

"I'm certain that he's hiding something." Luke walked down the hall in the direction of the holding cells. "The only questions are what, and why."

"I just want a few minutes, Luke, please!" Ally caught up with him and grabbed his arm. She turned him to face her. "You know that you can trust me."

"Of course I know that. But you need to keep in mind that if he's hiding things, it's because whatever he was up to, is worse than going back to prison for breaking his parole conditions. Don't let him con you." Luke locked his eyes to hers. "Understand?"

"Yes, I've got it." Ally looked through the bars of the nearby cell.

Tucker's slight frame was hunched over as he sat on a metal bench attached to the wall. She held her breath as a surge of empathy rushed through her. What if he had nothing to do with it? What if his mother, his only family, had just been murdered and he was the prime suspect for it, but he was innocent? She'd lost her own mother, but she couldn't imagine what Tucker might be feeling. It was one thing to lose a parent, it was quite another to be faced with that parent's murder.

"A few minutes." Luke's hand lingered on her back for a moment, then he turned and walked away. As he did, he nodded to the guard who sat at a desk not far from the holding cells.

"Tucker?" Ally wrapped her hands around two of the bars and leaned her head close to them. She spoke in a soft tone, so soft that she wasn't sure if he heard her at first.

"Go away." Tucker didn't look up.

"Tucker, it's Ally Sweet." She cleared her throat. "We've met a few times, when we were younger. You used to come into my grandmother's shop,

Charlotte's Chocolate Heaven. I know we don't really know each other well, but I'd like to talk with you. I'm trying to help you."

"Help me?" Tucker looked up at her, then quickly away. "Why would you want to do that?"

"Because I believe that you might be innocent, Tucker. But I can't prove that. You need to tell me where you were yesterday morning." Ally tried to meet his eyes, but he looked away before she could. "You're the only one that can help yourself."

"I can't help myself." Tucker ran his hands over his face and hunched his shoulders forward again. "There's no way to help myself. My mother is gone." A soft cry escaped his lips as he looked back up at her. "How could anyone do this to her?"

"I don't know, Tucker, but that's what I want to help find out." Ally tightened her grasp on the bars and pressed her forehead against them. "Where were you yesterday morning?"

"I still can't believe she's gone." Tucker winced, then squeezed his hands together between his knees. "You just have to let this happen." He looked up at her and met her eyes. "Just let it be, Ally. There's nothing else to do here. My mother died. The police are never going to listen to me. They won't believe anything I have to say. It's just how it is. There's no point in fighting it."

"I'll listen to you. If you are innocent you have to try and make them believe you." Ally narrowed her eyes, then took a sharp breath. "And more importantly, I believe your mother. I heard the pride in her voice when she talked about you. She knew that you were a good person, even with your mistakes, and she believed in you. I don't think you're a murderer. I don't think you're responsible for her death. I remember how close you were to her."

"Maybe I didn't kill her." Tucker cleared his throat, then looked back down at the floor. "But that doesn't mean I'm not responsible. You just don't understand, Ally."

"Then tell me." Ally let her hands slide down the bars as she sighed. "Please, help me to understand what's going through your mind, Tucker. Please, just let me help you."

"You can't help me. All right!" Tucker suddenly stood up from the bench and approached the bars. "I need you to leave me alone. I need you to stop coming here and telling me that there's some kind of hope, when there isn't. I don't care about going back to prison. I don't care about spending the rest of my life there. My life is over now. The one person who has always cared about me, who has always fought for me is gone. There's no point anymore."

"I know it might feel like that right now. But that's just not true." Ally's stomach churned as she recalled the pain she felt when her own mother had passed away. She was much younger than Tucker at the time, but she could still remember the pain it caused. "I know that your mother wouldn't want this for you. I know that it would break her heart to think that you got your second chance taken away because something terrible happened to her. So, you may not want my help, but I'm not going to go away. I'm going to do everything I can to find out the truth for your mother."

"Just leave me alone." Tucker slammed his palms against the bars so hard that the bars vibrated against Ally's palms.

Ally took a step back just as the guard stood up from his desk.

"Away from the bars!" He quickly walked over to Ally's side.

"It's okay." Ally took a breath as she stepped back. "Everything's fine." She held up her hands as she stared into Tucker's furious eyes. "I'm done here."

Ally turned and walked back down the hallway and out through the front doors of the police station. As the icy air struck her skin, she closed her eyes. Maybe Tucker hadn't murdered his mother, but there was a part of him that still blamed himself. The question was, why?

CHAPTER 9

*C*harlotte looked up from a pile of chocolates as the door of the shop swung open. She anticipated another wave of customers. Instead, she set eyes on Ally.

"Sorry, that took a little longer than I intended." Ally hurried behind the counter and took the tray of chocolates from her grandmother. "Where's Jeff?"

"I sent him home. He burnt chocolate." Charlotte clucked her tongue.

"I thought I smelled it a little." Ally scrunched up her nose. "Don't worry, he'll get the hang of it."

"Oh, I'm sure he will." Charlotte smiled. "It was sweet of him to help. But it's been a madhouse here. Did you get a chance to talk to Tucker?"

Before Ally could answer, another wave of

customers came in. Followed by a second, and third. By the time the shop emptied out, the sun had begun to set.

"Mee-Maw, you must be ready for a break." Ally frowned as she hugged her grandmother. "I didn't mean for you to be stuck here all day."

"Don't worry about that." Charlotte hugged her in return. "I loved being here with you. Why don't I pick up dinner and meet you at the cottage? We can discuss what you found out from Tucker."

"Sure, thanks Mee-Maw."

Charlotte left the shop and walked to the Chinese restaurant a few doors down. After ordering her food, she stepped outside to wait for it. She noticed a man huddled in the doorway of an empty shop across the street. His curls poked out from beneath a knit hat. She recalled moving him along from the door of the chocolate shop a few times already. This time though, she got a closer look at him. He was bundled in a coat, his hands were beet red from the cold. Charlotte's heart softened as she recognized the wear on his coat, and the hole in one of his shoes. She guessed that he might be homeless. It was rare to see a homeless person in the small town of Blue River. She crossed the street and dug her gloves out of her pocket.

"You look a little cold." Charlotte paused in front of him. "Would you like these? They're pink, but they're warm."

"Oh, thank you." His voice cracked as if he didn't speak often, as he took the gloves from her. "Oh, they're so soft. Did you make these?"

"It's a hobby I'm trying out." Charlotte smiled as she watched him tug them onto his hands. "Do you have somewhere to go, to get out of the cold?"

"I find places." He looked down at his hands. "Thank you so much, they were starting to go numb."

"You know there are some people who can help, I can take you to them if you'd like." Charlotte gazed at him.

"I don't need any help. Thanks for the gloves." He hurried past her, down the street.

Charlotte frowned as she walked back over to the Chinese restaurant. It didn't surprise her that he refused help. She knew that some homeless people were frightened by the thought of letting some of the government programs get involved in their lives, and others just preferred not to be noticed. She hoped he really did have somewhere warm to go.

After Charlotte picked up the food, she headed back to the cottage. She set the food in the kitchen, then opened the back door for Arnold and Peaches. Both of the animals loved to be outside, despite the cold, and she and Ally had created a nice fenced-in area for them that surrounded the now mostly dormant garden.

"Mee-Maw?" Ally's voice rang through the cottage.

"We're out back!" Charlotte smiled to herself. She never tired of hearing her granddaughter call out for her.

"That food smells wonderful." Ally stepped outside and hugged her. Then explained what she'd learned from both Luke, and Tucker. "We need to find out exactly where Tucker was, instead of at his parole meeting." Ally reached down to pat Arnold's head before he ran off through the yard. "Why didn't he go to his parole meeting? What is he hiding?"

"Ally, it's important to consider that it may not be something else that he's hiding. It may be that he really did commit this crime and that's why he doesn't have a good explanation about where he was." Charlotte shooed Peaches away from a spiderweb that stretched across one of the trees in the garden.

"I know that, I am keeping that in mind." Ally

shoved her hands into her pockets to warm them. "It's just hard for me to imagine that he could be capable of doing that, and around Christmas no less."

"Many people snap during the holidays. Louisa was so happy to have him home. Maybe he couldn't handle the pressure of that. Maybe she found out that he wasn't reformed." Charlotte cleared her throat. "Maybe when she said that she'd figured out who stole the money, she was talking about her son. Maybe she intended to turn him in, and he lost it, and killed her."

"Do you really think he stole the money from the mail truck?" Ally turned to face her. "I trust your instincts, Mee-Maw. I know he most likely would know all about the donation pick-ups. He probably would know her route, too. He could have easily accessed the mail truck. And you're right, if Louisa found out about it, even though she loved her son so much, she would have probably done the right thing and turned him in. I mean she turned him in before. But do you really think that Tucker did it?"

"He would have panicked at the thought of going back to prison. Maybe that's why he didn't show up to his meeting, because he thought it was pointless. He knew his mother was going to turn him in, and he would go back to prison. Maybe at first he surrendered to the idea, then he figured out there was another way to fix things. He probably had plans to go into hiding, but the murder was discovered before he could." Charlotte narrowed her eyes as she clapped her hands together. "It all adds up, doesn't it?"

"All, but the time of death." Ally leaned back against the fence and couldn't help but smile as Arnold dug himself a warm spot to nestle down in. "If Louisa was killed when the phone cut off, then she'd been dead for a few hours when Mrs. Bing showed up at her house. If he was the one who killed her, why would he still be in town? Why wouldn't he have taken off while he could?"

"That I don't have an answer for." Charlotte shook her head. "But then again, I can't fathom him wanting to kill his mother. Even if she is responsible for him going to prison in the first place, I still think it would have been too hard for him to do. We also don't know if Louisa was murdered at that time, or if the call just dropped."

"You're right. I asked Mrs. Bing about whether she saw Louisa's phone near her, and she said no. But she was also in shock, so she might have overlooked it. I'll check with Luke about it." Ally frowned. "I know there is a lot of evidence stacked up against Tucker, but I just don't think he did it." She sighed, then pulled her phone out of her pocket. "I just got a text from Luke. There's a press conference planned in an hour, to update the residents about the progress of the investigation."

"Sounds like we're going to have to eat fast." Charlotte corralled the animals towards the back door.

Ally and Charlotte managed to eat a couple of egg rolls and some sweet and sour chicken before they headed to the middle of town for the press conference.

Ally spotted Luke not far from the podium that had been set up in front of the police department entrance. The mayor had already begun to speak. As Ally walked up to Luke, he smiled at her.

Ally smiled in return then stood next to him and looked over at the mayor as she continued to speak. The crowd gathered in front of her, shouted questions, and appeared restless.

"This is not going to go well." Luke straightened his collar, then looked in the direction of the crowd.

"You can't turn back time, you can only do your job." Ally turned to look at the angry faces in the crowd. Luke wasn't wrong. The same people that had wished her a Merry Christmas over the past few days, looked as if they were out for blood. She couldn't blame them either. The entire town was in an uproar over first a horrible theft, and then an unspeakable tragedy. Things like that, didn't happen in Blue River and just weren't supposed to happen during the holidays.

Ally watched as Luke walked up to the podium. Silence briefly fell over the crowd as he began to speak.

"I'd like to give an update on the investigation before we start." Luke cleared his throat, then gripped the top of the podium as he looked out at the sea of faces.

Ally took a position near the rear of the crowd. She wanted to get a good look at who was there. Would a thief and a murderer show up to a press conference that was about him? She wasn't sure, but she wanted to get an idea of how people were reacting, and whether anyone behaved in a strange or unexpected way.

"At this time, we have been able to determine that this was most likely an isolated incident. The people of Blue River do not need to be afraid that this could happen to them."

"What makes it an isolated incident?" A woman in her fifties near the rear of the crowd called out. Ally recognized her as Doris. She was in the same book club as her grandmother. "How am I supposed to know that this isn't going to happen to me?"

"Due to the evidence at the scene, we believe this was a targeted attack. At this time, we can only assume that the attack was personal," Luke replied.

"That's not good enough. Assumptions aren't good enough." A man towards the front of the crowd threw his fist into the air. Ally tried to see if she knew him, but the crowd was blocking him from view. "Maybe there is a psychopath on the loose that is murdering people. You can't prove there isn't, can you?"

"Sir, please, allow me to take care of the investigation. I can assure you that if I thought there was any risk to anyone else in this community, I would make everyone aware of that." Luke held up his hands. "What we need now, is for people to remain calm. We need people to come forward, with any information that they might have, no matter how small. Did you notice anyone acting strangely towards Louisa? Did you happen to see something odd near her home? Did you overhear a conversation that made you uneasy? All of this information can go far to helping us complete this investigation. Please do not be afraid to come forward if you think you may have seen or heard something that could help us."

"I didn't see or hear anything other than a crime wave breaking out in what is supposed to be a safe town." A young man who stood towards the front of the crowd stepped right up to the podium and stared into Luke's eyes. "Maybe if you were a little more proactive with your policing, Louisa would still be here. Didn't you even think to warn her that it was a bad idea to travel with that much money in her vehicle? Did you ever offer her security so that she could feel safe while doing a kind act for others? Did you notice anyone following her? Did you see anything odd near her house? You sure didn't keep Louisa safe, how are we supposed to believe that you are going to do anything to keep us safe?"

Ally walked around the side of the crowd to look at him. She recognized him as Tobias, a regular at Charlotte's Chocolate Heaven.

"I understand your concern." Luke took a deep breath, then looked back out at the crowd. "At a time like this, it can be very easy to point fingers and make accusations, but the most important thing to remember is that we have lost a beloved member of our community, and she deserves justice. We can't find that by tearing each other apart. We can only give her the justice she deserves by working together, and supporting each other, as we try to get through this terrible time. We are first and foremost a community, one I am very proud to be a part of." He clenched his jaw, then shook his head. "All I can do is try to serve Louisa, and the rest of this community, by solving the crime that took her from us. Someone here, or someone that you know who isn't here, knows something. We just need to get to that person and find that piece of information that will give us a solid lead to follow. Don't underestimate your ability to make a difference in this investigation." He took a slight step back from the podium. "That is all I have to offer at the moment. We will be answering phones twenty-four hours a day, and the police station will be open at all hours. If you want to come forward with any information, please don't hesitate."

Ally bit into her bottom lip as she watched him walk away from the podium. She knew that he wouldn't rest until the murder was solved. She would do anything to help speed that process along.

CHAPTER 10

Charlotte spent some time in front of the mirror the next morning. Over the years she had begun to use a little more makeup here and there, just to cover up the wrinkles and the age spots. But today, she used even more. She felt like she needed a boost after everything that had happened.

After getting ready, Charlotte headed for the chocolate shop. She wanted to check in with Ally. When she stepped inside, she found her nearly hidden by a stack of chocolate boxes.

"Ally, are you back there?" Charlotte laughed.

"I'm back here." Ally peeked around the boxes. "I'm almost caught up with the orders, but there are plenty more to start on."

"How are you doing today?" Charlotte walked around behind the counter.

"I'm okay." Ally frowned. "I was up most of the night trying to figure this all out."

"I was afraid of that." Charlotte crossed her arms. "Any ideas?"

"I think the only thing we can do is figure out exactly where Louisa was the morning of her death. Maybe if we follow her routine, we can turn up something that was out of place." Ally sighed as she met her eyes. "It's not much, I know."

"Re-tracing her final steps is a good idea." Charlotte hugged Ally, then pulled away and looked into her eyes. "But I'd like to do it."

"Why?" Ally smiled.

"I think that people might be more forthcoming with giving me information because I am not dating a detective." Charlotte gazed into her eyes. "You handle the shop and keep following up leads about Tucker. We still need to know where he was yesterday."

"Okay." Ally took a deep breath. "Thanks, Mee-Maw."

"Anytime." Charlotte smiled.

"Those are the boxes of orders that still need to

be collected." Ally pointed to a large pile of boxes. "There is still a lot to do."

"Wow." Charlotte's eyes widened. "You've been busy."

"Which is great." Ally smiled.

"I'll be back soon."

"Bye Mee-Maw." Ally waved as Charlotte turned and walked out of the shop.

As the cold air bit into Charlotte's cheeks, she lowered her head against the wind. The air was crisp, but also damp. Her heart skipped a beat as she realized that snow was coming. Never once did her nose steer her wrong in the past. As soon as she detected that certain combination of moisture and cold in the air, she knew that snow was brewing. She sighed as she looked up at the heavy clouds in the sky. She doubted it would be a flurry. How would a snowstorm impact the murder investigation? She headed for the bakery, where she knew that Louisa started out her route every morning. The bakery was a gathering place for most of the early risers and some of the older residents of Blue River that moved on to the chocolate shop later in the day when it opened.

They started out their day with a cup of coffee, some pastries and a chat, sometimes even before the sun came up, or right after. Louisa was one of the earliest who arrived. Charlotte could recall times when she would find Louisa walking out with her coffee and pastry, just as she arrived to order some breakfast for her and Ally when they had an early morning start at the shop. Louisa took her job very seriously, and never ran late.

"Morning Robin." Charlotte smiled at the new assistant behind the counter. Over the years many new employees had been hired and had moved on. Robin was one of the newest. The young woman looked barely over eighteen, but Charlotte knew she was in her twenties. She knew she'd come to Blue River to get away from a bad relationship, and she'd yet to find her footing in the town. "How are you doing today?"

"Pretty good." Robin smiled in return. "What can I get for you?"

"Two bagels, please." Charlotte glanced up at the clock on the wall. "I know I'm a little later than usual."

"Not much." Robin grinned as she got the bagels.

"I was wondering, did you see Louisa in here yesterday?" Charlotte frowned. "I came in for bagels, but I don't recall seeing her."

"Oh, she came in extra early." Robin set down the bagels in front of Charlotte. "I had just unlocked the doors in fact. She was in a hurry, too."

"Really? Did she say why she was in a rush? Thanks for this." Charlotte picked up the bagels and left some money on the counter.

"She said she had some extra packages, that had to be hand delivered, and signed for. She knew that would take a little extra time, so she decided to get an even earlier start than usual." Robin shook her head as she rested her hands on the counter. Her eyes shifted towards the ceiling and she sighed. "It's hard to believe that was the last time I saw her."

"I know, it's tough for all of us to believe it." Charlotte frowned, then set her cup down without taking a sip. "Did she say anything else about the packages? Like who they were for?"

"No nothing." Robin shrugged, then waved to another customer who walked in. "She didn't say who they were going to. I wish I had taken a little extra time to talk with her. She showed me a picture of the Christmas tree that she put up with her son." Her cheeks flushed as her smile spread wider. "I made some comment about how cute he was, and then she decided she was going to try to set us up. She warned me that he had been in some trouble, but that he'd turned over a new leaf." She looked into Charlotte's eyes. "I told her I know what it's like to make mistakes. She seemed to be really happy about that."

"It must have been a very sweet picture." Charlotte's heart warmed at the thought. Did a son who was planning to murder his mother, decorate a Christmas tree with her the day before? She doubted it. What could have happened between the time that they decorated for the holidays together, and the moment that Louisa had been killed? She had to admit, that she understood why Ally had become pretty much convinced that Tucker was not involved.

"It was a sweet picture, and a sweet moment that they shared. Honestly, I've never met him, but I've been a little worried about him. Do you think that he'll be released soon?" Robin lowered her voice. "It didn't seem like the police had much to go on at the press conference last night."

"I really don't know." Charlotte frowned. "What I do know, is that I hope the killer is found."

"Me too." Robin snapped her fingers. "Oh, I do remember one thing. She bought six cinnamon rolls. She said they were her friend Jen's favorite, and she wanted to drop them by the library. Does that help?"

"Yes, it does." Charlotte smiled at her. "Thank you so much."

Ally spent most of her morning and early afternoon working on orders and helping customers. She managed to get a few texts off to Luke, but he barely responded. She could only imagine how busy he was. He did reply that Louisa's phone was found near her body which indicated to Ally that the call to Mrs. Bing cut off because Louisa was about to be murdered. As the afternoon transitioned to evening, the frequency of customers began to slow some. She noticed a boy walk through the door. He had spiky, brown hair, and she recognized him from a visit to the shop the previous day.

"Hello again?" She smiled at him as he looked over the assortment of chocolates on display. "Are you still looking for a gift for your mother?"

"Yes." He glanced up at her with a faint smile. "It's hard to find just the right thing."

"You might like some of the wooden toys that we have, or the statues. As an added touch your mother could paint them herself." Ally pointed out the items on the shelves near him.

"That's a good idea. She's pretty creative. I'll take a look." He began to walk along the shelves that contained the carved items. Ally treasured every one of them, because she knew that Luke had created them. While the boy looked for the right item, she grabbed another tray of chocolates and slid on some gloves, so that she could fill up some boxes. When the shop phone rang, she took off a glove and snatched it up.

"Charlotte's Chocolate Heaven, this is Ally, can I help you?"

"Oh, I was trying to reach Charlotte." The voice on the other end of the phone sounded unfamiliar to Ally.

"I'm her granddaughter, is there anything I can help you with?" Ally turned to the back counter so that she could organize the boxes she had already filled.

"She told me to call this number if I found out anything about Tucker." She hesitated. "Maybe I should call back?"

"No, please don't call back. I'd like to hear anything you might know." Ally pressed the phone tighter against her ear.

"Ally, it's Ashley from Polly's Place."

"Oh, sorry Ashley, I didn't recognize your voice." Ally smiled.

"No problem. I had mentioned to Charlotte that I thought Tucker was acting frightened, and today I ran into a mutual friend. He told me that ever since Tucker was released, one of the guys he got arrested with has been following him around and giving him a hard time. I don't know what the whole story is, but I guess that he wanted something from Tucker. His name is James Carlo. Maybe that will help?" Ashley sighed. "I hate to think that Tucker is in some kind of trouble."

"Thanks a lot for the information. I'll look into it right away. If you hear anything else, please don't hesitate to call." Ally hung up the phone, and turned around to face the shop just in time to see the boy tuck one of the larger wooden statues into his jacket.

"Wait a minute, you need to pay for that!" Startled, Ally tried to convince herself that it was a simple mistake.

But the boy bolted out through the door without a second glance.

"Hey! Get back here!" Ally ran around the counter and through the front door. She caught a glimpse of him as he raced down the sidewalk. She hesitated long enough to lock the shop door, then took off after him. As she ran as fast as she could the cold air blasted against her skin. She hadn't taken the time to put on her coat. The air smelled like snow. She hunched up her shoulders and shivered as she searched the sidewalk for any sign of the boy. She caught a glimpse of his blue coat just as he rounded the corner of the main street. She ran even faster, determined not to let him get away. She had no idea what she might do with him when she caught him, but she didn't want one of Luke's pieces to be stolen.

Ally rounded the corner, but her foot caught on something against the wall and sent her flying to the ground. As her arm struck the hard pavement, she heard a gasp and a gurgle and felt something soft under her torso. It took her a few seconds to realize that she hadn't just landed on the ground, she'd landed partially on top of someone.

As Ally scrambled to her feet, the man beneath her pushed aside the cardboard he'd been laying under.

"I'm so sorry!" Ally smoothed down her shirt and stared down at the man as he sat up. "Are you okay? Did I hurt you?"

"I'm fine I think." He ran his pink gloves across his face. "Where are you going in such a hurry?"

"I'm just trying to catch up to someone." Ally crouched down in front of him. "Are you sure you're okay? I landed pretty hard."

"I'm tough." He chuckled. "Glad I was able to break your fall." He met her eyes. "It's not every day a pretty lady falls for me, you know?"

Ally smiled a little at his joke, then looked over the cardboard he'd pushed aside. "Are you sleeping out here?"

"Don't worry, I'll move on." He started to get to his feet. "No need to call the police."

"I'm not going to call the police." Ally smiled. "I just think you might be better off in the local shelter. It's supposed to get so cold tonight. Can I take you there?"

"No, thanks. I'm just fine on my own." He eyed her. "You're not going to call the police?"

"No, I won't. But if you stay here, I'll bring you some food and blankets by tonight. Okay?" Ally frowned as she looked up at the sky. "It sure looks like it's going to snow tonight."

"I have places to go to get out of the bad weather if I need to. Don't worry." He cleared his throat. "Thank you for your kindness, miss. I'll be here."

"Okay." Ally stared at him a moment longer, then looked down the street in the direction the boy had fled. There wasn't much chance she would catch him now, but she still wanted to try. As she hurried down the street, she heard a shout from not too far ahead of her. She watched as a motorcycle bolted out from behind a building and tore into the street. As the motorcycle flew by her, she caught sight of flowing red hair beneath the helmet the rider wore. She jogged towards the back of the building where she'd heard the shout. As she reached it, she saw a man disappear around the corner of another building.

"Well, I'm just getting nowhere at the moment." Ally sighed as she turned back in the direction of the shop. At the very least she could make sure the man she'd tripped over was warm and had some hot soup and bread to enjoy. She stopped at the grocery store near the end of the street and picked out a few thick blankets. She grabbed a loaf of bread, some peanut butter, and a bottle of water.

After making her purchases, she stopped by Polly's Place. After her eyes adjusted to the bright lights inside, she ordered a large serving of soup. On her way back to the spot where she'd seen the man, she spotted a boy in a blue jacket. He looked like the same boy that ran from the shop. She watched as he stepped inside the jewelry store. Seconds later, Nancy, the owner of the jewelry store, stepped out, with her hand around the boy's arm.

"Mom, I'm sorry I was late!" The boy huffed.

"Sorry doesn't always cut it, Cody." Nancy slammed the door shut, and locked it, then steered the boy towards a nearby car.

Ally's heart pounded. She knew that she could confront the woman and her son, but she had no way to prove that he'd stolen anything. Now that she knew who his mother was, she intended to have a conversation with her. But it would have to wait, as she didn't want the man's soup to get cold.

When Ally returned to him, she found him in the same place, with the cardboard pulled up over him again.

"Here, I got you a few things to help you through the night." Ally handed him over the cup of soup and placed the bag of items beside him. "I know it's not much."

"It's everything." He smiled up at her. "I'm Rodney by the way."

"I'm Ally." She studied him. "I've seen you around. If you ever need any help, just stop by

Charlotte's Chocolate Heaven, okay?" She pointed towards the chocolate shop.

"Sure, I'll do that. Thanks again." Rodney took a big whiff of the soup and sighed.

"Please, try to stay warm." Ally smiled, then headed back towards the shop.

CHAPTER 11

*C*harlotte stepped into the library and her nostrils immediately flared. She took another breath, then covered her nose. Confused by the scent that permeated the library, she made her way towards the librarian's desk.

"Jen, what's happened in here?" She lowered her hand as she looked at the woman behind the desk.

"I know it smells a little." Jen scrunched up her nose as she moved an air freshener closer to the edge of her desk. "I guess that's the price we all have to pay for the brand-new carpet. Kevin said it would only take a few days for the smell to disappear, but it's already been a few days." She sighed, then shrugged. "There's not much we can do about it now. If it wasn't so cold out, I would open all the windows, but that isn't an option at the moment. Did you hear about the snow coming in?"

"Yes, I did. Hopefully, it will only be an inch or two. If it's more than that this whole place will grind to a halt." Charlotte rolled her eyes as she laughed. "That's the last thing we need during the Christmas rush."

"So true. But it might mean a few days off for me." Jen smiled as she shuffled some papers on her desk. "And believe me, I could use it." Her smile faded. She sat back in her chair. "After what happened to Louisa, I'm not feeling very festive."

"I imagine not." Charlotte rested her hands on the desk and leaned closer to her. "I'm so sorry for your loss. I know you two were close."

"Not terribly close. But I did appreciate how hard she worked. And, I was hoping to help her son out." Jen narrowed her eyes and drew her lips into a thin line. She let a breath out between her lips. "To think that I almost hired him here. And look what he did to his mother."

"Allegedly. He hasn't been charged yet." Charlotte offered the word in a soft tone and tried to meet Jen's eyes. "It was kind of you to try to help him. Not many people would take a chance on a felon."

"I believed Louisa when she said that her son was reformed. I really did." Jen pursed her lips, then shook her head. "I just can't figure out how he could have done this. You say allegedly, but it's already all around town that he lied to the police, and he had a problem with his mother."

"Rumors spread quickly around here, but that doesn't necessarily make them true. I'm hoping to find out a little bit more about what Louisa was up to on her last day." Charlotte adjusted her purse on her shoulder.

"Oh, are you trying to help work out who did this, like usual?" Jen asked.

"I guess." Charlotte shrugged. Ally and Charlotte had quite the reputation for investigating mysteries.

"Well, I did see her." Jen stood up from her chair and walked around to the front of the desk. "She gave me some cinnamon rolls. I told her, she didn't have to, but she insisted. She said she liked spoiling people. She often brought me treats." She pressed her hand against her stomach as she looked towards the floor. "When I heard about what happened, all I could do was think about how kind she was. Always thinking of others."

"She was very special." Charlotte took her hand and gave it a light squeeze.

"Yes, yes she was." Jen drew a deep breath. "I wish it never happened, but there's nothing we can do about that, right?"

"Unfortunately, no." Charlotte swept her gaze over the nearly empty library. "I guess the cold is keeping people away?"

"The cold, and the holiday tasks." Jen shrugged.

"What happened here?" Charlotte eyed a big circular stain on the brand-new carpet. "A spill?"

"It's such a reminder of Louisa." Jen smiled some as she looked at the stain. "When she came in here to give me the cinnamon rolls, she had her mailbag packed full of small boxes. When she tried to pull out the cinnamon rolls and my mail, one of the boxes fell out and hit the floor. It had a bottle of perfume in it, and the bottle broke. The perfume seeped through the box and spilled all over the carpet. She felt so badly. I told her not to worry about it, that I could clean it up for her, but she insisted. She got down on her knees with a rag and some spray and tried to scrub it all out of the carpet. She even took the broken perfume bottle in the box with her." She frowned as she continued to study the circle on the carpet. "It looked good when she first cleaned it, but I guess the oil or something in the perfume left a residue. Kevin said he'd come back out and pull the stain out, but to be honest with you, I'd rather he didn't. It reminds me of her so much. She was always so quick to take on responsibility."

"I can just see her now, down there scrubbing." Charlotte shook her head as she smiled. "She would have been determined to get it clean."

"At least she thought she did clean it up. She didn't have that on her mind." Jen looked up at her. "That's something, isn't it?"

"It certainly is." Charlotte nodded. "Did she say anything about where she was going after she left the library?"

"She had to finish delivering the rest of the boxes. They were going to the jewelry store. I guess to be part of some kind of promotion. After that, she said she'd go home to have lunch then finish the rest of the deliveries. She was still so rattled by the theft of the charity money. I tried to tell her it wasn't her fault, but I don't think she believed me." Jen raised one finger in the air. "Actually, she did mention that she planned to make some cookies with Tucker. She thought that would brighten up her evening." She let her hand fall back to her side as she narrowed her eyes. "Do you really think he baked with her and then killed her?"

"I hope not." Charlotte pressed her hand against her chest. "I'd rather think that's not even possible."

"So would I, but if you watch the news you'll see these terrible things happen every day. I guess it was naive of all of us to believe that it couldn't happen here." Jen glanced at the front door as a young man who Charlotte recognized as Sam, the owner of the dry cleaners, stepped inside. "I guess there are a few stragglers who still want books." She smiled as she looked back at Charlotte. "How is business this holiday season?"

"Busy." Charlotte narrowed her eyes. "I would like this murder solved so at least that can be put to rest and the community can feel safe again. So, Louisa didn't mention having any trouble with Tucker?"

"No, not at all. Her face lit up every time she talked about him." Jen shrugged. "I would expect her to hold some resentment towards him for all he put her through, but it was like she had totally forgiven him. I guess it's good that she didn't have that on her mind either. We can hope that she had no idea who her killer was."

"Yes, we can hope that. Thanks for your time." Charlotte smiled, then headed for the door. As she stepped out into the cold, her heart grew heavy with the knowledge that Louisa probably did know who her killer was. She had figured out who had stolen the money from the mail truck. If that person found out, he or she would have plenty of reason to want Louisa dead. Was it Tucker? Without an alibi, there was no way to rule him out.

Ally was relieved to be home, and excited to be greeted at the door by Arnold and Peaches. She set her keys down on the counter and headed into the kitchen to prepare dinner for a pig, and a cat. As she began getting their dishes together, she thought about the call from her grandmother. She had managed to track Louisa's movements during her last shift that she didn't even get to finish, but it hadn't revealed much. The way everyone continued to emphasize how much Louisa loved her son, created conflict in Ally. Yes, it was possible that he had his mother fooled, but it was also possible that an innocent, grieving man was locked away for a crime he didn't commit.

Ally grabbed her phone and made a call to Mrs. Bing.

"Ally, any news?" She asked quickly.

"Unfortunately, not much just yet. I was wondering though, do you know anything about Nancy, the owner of the jewelry store?" Ally poured food into Peaches' bowl.

"Only that she lives in Mainbry, and that her store was robbed a short time ago."

"What about her son Cody? Do you know anything about him?" Ally added food to Arnold's bowl, as he squealed enthusiastically.

"Again, not much. He was living with his dad in another state but moved to Mainbry to live with his mom a couple of months ago. He spends quite a bit of time at the jewelry store with his mom. I have heard a few of the other parents mention that he's been in a bit of trouble at school. But I guess it's hard for him to adjust to a move in the middle of the school year."

"Yes, you're probably right about that." Ally

frowned. "Thanks Mrs. Bing. You have a good night."

"You too, Ally. Let me know if there's anything I can do to help with the investigation. And make sure you keep me in the loop."

"I will." Ally ended the call. As she gave Arnold and Peaches their food, her stomach rumbled. She'd been so caught up in the murder and the shop that she'd barely had anything to eat herself. She was about to pull a frozen meal out of the freezer when she heard a light knock on the door.

"Ally?" Luke poked his head inside.

"Luke!" Ally smiled as she walked over to him. "Is this an official visit?"

"Officially, I am having a break before I go back to the station." Luke stepped into the cottage and held up a paper bag. "I owe you dinner."

"I'm not sure if that's true, I think it's me that owes you." Ally grinned as she took the bag and carried it into the kitchen.

"Either way, I'm here for some quality Ally time."

Ally hugged Luke and gave him a quick kiss on the lips. The tenderness in his eyes made her heart skip a beat.

Arnold left his food and ran over to greet Luke.

"And pig time. Hi buddy." Luke had originally taken some time to get used to the pot-bellied pig, but they had become good friends. Ally smiled at the interaction. Luke crouched down to stroke Arnold behind the ear. Then he walked towards the table as Arnold walked back to his food bowl. Peaches didn't raise her head from her bowl. Food always came first for Peaches.

Luke sat down at the table as Ally opened up the bag.

"How is Tucker doing?" Ally pulled the food out of the bag.

"Ally time, not work time." Luke groaned.

"I'm sorry." Ally grabbed them each a bottle of water from the fridge. "I'm just so preoccupied with all of this. Did you know that he was frightened of the man he committed the burglary with? His name is James Carlo. Apparently, James has been giving him a hard time since he's been out."

"We have looked into James, Tucker did more time than James and James was out before him, but he claims that he didn't have any contact with Tucker since his release. Tucker claims the same thing." Luke shrugged. "Until we can prove otherwise, we have to take him at his word."

"What if someone saw him with James?" Ally met his eyes.

"If that person came forward, it would change things. There is one thing Tucker has been cleared of, if that helps." Luke cracked open his bottle of water. "We do have an alibi for him for the time of the theft of the charity money."

"Really?" Ally sat down across from him, her eyes wide. "That changes everything."

"How?" Luke raised an eyebrow.

"Wait, where was he?" Ally opened her own water as her mind raced.

"He was at a job interview at a factory on the outskirts of town. I confirmed the time with the interviewer, and also with the timestamp on their camera." Luke pointed to the food in front of her. "Eat it while it's warm, burgers don't taste good otherwise."

"I am, I am." Ally took a small bite. "So, this shows two things. He really was trying to turn his life around, and he had no motive to want to kill his mother. If he had stolen the money, and she found out about it, then it would explain why he did it, but he didn't steal the money, we know that now."

"We know that, yes. But that doesn't clear him of the murder. He still can't, or won't, tell us where he was at the time of the murder. In fact, thanks to Mrs. Bing, we can confirm that his truck was nearby when she found Louisa. He drives a red truck, she identified one near the house and we used traffic cameras to confirm it. But he still won't admit that he was there. Why wasn't he at his parole meeting?" Luke rolled his eyes. "Honestly, I think he just wants us to lock him up and throw away the key. You'd think that would make my job easier, but it really doesn't. Instead, I have to question everything at least twice." He picked up a french fry. "And I came here to get away from this, remember?"

"I'm sorry, Luke." Ally reached across the table and rubbed the back of his hand. "I promise, no more talk about work."

"Good." Luke locked his eyes to hers. "Seeing you is always the best part of my day."

"Mine too." Ally smiled.

Ally spent the next hour chatting with him about everything other than the case, despite the fact that she had a million questions about it burning in her mind. By the time he went back to work, she was ready for bed. As she tried to sleep, thoughts of what Tucker might be hiding kept her awake. If he wasn't the one who stole the money, then who was?

Her thoughts turned back to Cody. He was often at his mother's store. What if he had seen Louisa pick up the money from the donation jar at the jewelry store? Maybe he had followed her and taken the opportunity to steal the money? She couldn't let that go. She had to talk to Nancy.

CHAPTER 12

First thing in the morning, before she opened the chocolate shop, Ally headed for the jewelry store.

"Excuse me?" Ally walked up to the door, just as Nancy stepped out.

"Ally." Nancy turned to face her, with a large bag in one hand, and her purse clutched in the other. "We're closed for about another hour, but if you can come back, I'd be happy to show you anything you might be interested in."

"Actually, that's not why I'm here." Ally squeezed the strap of her purse and tried to meet Nancy's eyes. "It's about your son."

"My son?" Nancy asked.

"I need to discuss an incident that happened with your son."

"What kind of incident?" Nancy scowled. "My son isn't even here today, he's at school."

"This actually happened yesterday." Ally straightened her shoulders. "He stole an item from my shop."

"Oh, you must be mistaken!" Nancy laughed loudly. "My son would never steal anything. He's a good boy."

"I'm sure he is." Ally lowered her voice. "Which is why I thought I'd come to you to discuss this matter, because I don't want any rumors getting around town. I have no interest in involving law enforcement. But I would like what he stole back."

"I'm sorry, you think that you're going to walk up to my store and accuse my son of doing something, and I'm just going to believe you?" Nancy shook her head. "My son is not a thief, and I am offended that you would even suggest it. I don't know if you're just making something up, or if you misunderstood something that happened, but you are certainly out of your mind if you think that I am going to take anything you say seriously."

"I had hoped that we could be civil about this. I saw him take it with my own eyes, and I saw him run to your store. Now, if we can't settle this like neighbors, then I will have to pursue other options. The statue he stole was not exactly cheap, but I am willing to overlook the entire incident as long as he returns it." Ally held out a business card to her. "This has my cell phone number as well. Please contact me if you change your mind. Otherwise, I will have to take the next step."

"The next step?" Nancy's cheeks flushed as she glared at her. "What exactly is the next step?"

"I will be forced to file a police report." Ally crossed her arms.

"You are dating a cop, aren't you?" Nancy nodded slowly. "Detective Luke Elm."

"I am, but who I'm dating is not relevant." Ally frowned as her patience began to run thin. "You have my contact information. I'm sorry, I understand that this is very upsetting for you, but it is upsetting for me, too. I'm sure your son is a very lovely young man, but I need that statue back." She wanted to ask where he was when the donation money was stolen from the mail truck, but she didn't want to antagonize the woman further.

"I have to go." Nancy glared at Ally, then pushed past her. She tossed the bag into her car, then settled in the front seat. She poked her head out the window long enough to meet Ally's eyes. "If I see you anywhere near my store, or my son, I will have you charged with harassment." With that she screeched away from the curb.

Ally sighed as she watched her go. She hadn't intended to upset the woman, but she had needed to discuss the missing statue with her.

On her way back to the shop, Ally peeked down the alley where she'd seen Rodney the night before. She saw no sign of him, but his cardboard and a few things were still there. She hoped that he might have decided to go to a shelter to stay warm. Or even had another warm place to stay. As she unlocked the door of the shop, she sensed a presence behind her. Before she could turn, a hand landed on her shoulder.

"I could use some help."

Ally jumped and jerked away from the touch. As she locked eyes with the man who had touched her, her heart raced.

"Rodney. You can't sneak up on people like that."

"Oh, I'm so sorry." Rodney lowered his eyes. "I didn't mean to frighten you. I just wondered if maybe I could have a cup of coffee."

"That's okay, of course." Ally smiled, then

opened the door to let him inside. "I still have to make some. It'll be a few minutes."

"Oh, that's all right, I'll just have a look around." Rodney wandered down the aisles.

Ally fought the urge to wonder if he might steal something. She knew it wasn't right to judge him just because he was homeless. Still, as she started the coffee, she kept her eye on him.

"Such beautiful work." Rodney ran his fingertips across one of Luke's bigger pieces, a large wooden clock. "An artist made this."

"My boyfriend actually. His name is Luke. He's a police detective." Ally cleared her throat. "Did you go to the shelter last night?"

"I can't go to those places." Rodney huffed. "They are full of thieves."

"I'm sure that's not entirely true." Ally poured him a cup of coffee, then put out a tray of cream and sugar, as well as a few chocolates and cookies. "Here, sit in here and warm up for a bit."

"Thank you." Rodney smiled. "You are such a kind person. Like my own Christmas miracle."

Ally blushed at his words. "I wish I could do more."

"You've done more than you'll ever know." Rodney winked at her, then took a sip of his coffee.

"Don't let me hold you up, I'm sure you have plenty of work to do."

Ally began to sort through the orders for the day.

"Have you been around here long?"

"About a month or so." Rodney picked up one of the cookies.

"Were you around when the mail truck was robbed?" Ally straightened up as she turned to look at him.

"I was around." Rodney narrowed his eyes. "Why?"

"I'm just curious." Ally shrugged. "Did you notice anyone hanging around it?"

"The police already asked me about it. I didn't do it." Rodney stood up suddenly. "I didn't steal anything!"

"It's okay." Ally held up her hands as she noted the panic in his eyes. "I wasn't accusing you."

"Yes, you were! You're just like everyone else! Keep your coffee!" Rodney glared at her. "I told the police, and I'll tell you the same thing, it was the man in the red truck! He's the one that stole that money!" He turned and stormed out of the shop.

Ally stared after him, stunned not only by the

way he'd reacted, but also by his words. The man in the red truck? A red truck like the one Tucker drove? If he was across town at a job interview, then how was his truck near his mother's mail truck?

Ally didn't have much time to consider it before Mrs. Bing, Mrs. White, and Mrs. Cale walked through the door.

"Good morning, ladies." Ally forced a smile as she cleaned up the still half-full coffee cup and left-behind candies. "I just made a pot of coffee if you'd like some."

"Absolutely." Mrs. Bing plopped down on one of the bar stools in front of the counter.

"Mrs. Bing, did Luke tell you that the truck you spotted near Louisa's house likely belonged to Tucker?" Ally handed her a cup of coffee.

"Yes, he did." Mrs. Bing picked up the cream to add some. "Why?"

"It's just hard for me to believe he was there." Ally sighed. "Every time I think we're getting closer to clearing him, even more evidence against him crops up."

"Ally, if he was there, why would he leave if he was innocent?" Mrs. Bing shook her head. "I know you have a soft spot for the boy, but what explanation could he have for lying about being there and then leaving before the police arrived?"

"I have no idea." Ally handed Mrs. White and Mrs. Cale cups of coffee as well. "I'd like to believe that there is one, but I don't know what it would be."

"That's up to Tucker to provide, right?" Mrs. Bing shrugged, then turned to the other two women beside her. "What do you two think about this?"

"It's hard to say." Mrs. White narrowed her eyes. "If his truck was there, I'd say he was up to something."

"He certainly wouldn't have been sitting in it for no reason. It's too cold to be outside." Mrs. Cale shivered and tucked her hands into the fluffy pockets on her jacket.

"It's not so bad." Mrs. White unwrapped her scarf. "Not as bad as it was four winters ago, that's for sure."

"It's bad enough." Mrs. Cale shivered.

"No snow yet, though." Ally held out the sample tray to the three women. "We have plenty of white chocolate coconut stars."

"Yum!" Mrs. Cale gathered up a few.

"Mrs. Bing?" Ally turned back to her. "You

noticed the red truck near Louisa's house before you went inside, right?"

"Yes, I did. I think it drew my attention because it was an unusual color." Mrs. Bing grabbed a white chocolate coconut star. "Why?"

"Do you recall noticing it any other time? Like around the time that Louisa's mail truck was robbed?" Ally leaned against the counter and looked into the woman's eyes.

"Actually, yes!" Mrs. Bing's eyes widened. "I do remember seeing it. I had just shooed away that pesky vagabond that always wants my loose change, and when I looked up, I saw this bright red truck pull up behind the mail truck. I thought it would blare it's horn since the truck was stopped, but it didn't."

"Did you see anyone get out of the truck?" Ally's eyes widened.

"No, I was too busy trying to get away from that man." Mrs. Bing winced. "I wish Luke would do something about him, get him out of our town."

"Mrs. Bing, that's so harsh." Mrs. White glared at her. "He's just down on his luck."

"Down on his luck, my right toe!" Mrs. Bing huffed. "He knows how to play the part to get people to feel sorry for him, that's all. Some of these bums have huge bank accounts."

"Nonsense." Mrs. Cale snapped. "It's Christmas, you shouldn't talk like that."

"The truth is the truth, all year round!" Mrs. Bing picked up another candy.

"He seemed nice enough to me." Ally frowned. "But it might be best to keep your distance from him." She recalled how quickly he'd gotten upset that morning. Maybe Rodney was a little dangerous, but he was also right. The red truck had been there at the time of the theft, which meant that he might have seen the thief.

CHAPTER 13

"*M*orning." Charlotte stepped through the door of the shop and smiled at the three women at the counter. "You beat me here today."

"Perfect timing." Mrs. White rolled her eyes. "We could use a level head in this debate."

"Oh?" Charlotte grinned as she walked around the counter to hug Ally. "I'm not sure I can contribute that, but I can try."

"Actually, I've been meaning to ask you about the homeless man, Rodney." Ally hugged her, then looked into her eyes. "What did you say to him the other day when he was in front of the shop?"

"I asked him to move along." Charlotte shrugged.

"See?" Mrs. Bing snapped her fingers. "Charlotte knows that it's not good to have a bum hanging out outside your shop."

"I never said that." Charlotte narrowed her eyes. "Yes, I asked him to move along because it's not good for business for him to be peering through the window. I've warned him before that if he's going to be out front of the shop, he needs to give the customers space, and he needs to try not to scare them. But whenever I ask him to move on, I do so by giving him a twenty and sending him to the diner." She shook her head. "I would never sweep him away like dirt on the sidewalk."

"Don't you see that you're enabling him?" Mrs. Bing sighed. "Of course, he's going to keep coming back to get that twenty."

"What I see is a man who has lost his way. I don't know his story, but I do know that no one should be living a life where there is nowhere to turn, and no one to turn to. Not all of us are lucky enough to have the support of family and friends." Charlotte donned an apron and walked over to the sink. As she turned on the faucet, she glanced back at Mrs. Bing. "Sometimes life can be endlessly harsh."

"Maybe, but sometimes a person can be that

cruel as well. Have we even considered that not long after this bum." Mrs. Bing paused and rolled her eyes as Mrs. Cale gave her a light poke. "This Rodney fellow arrived in our town, the petty crimes began to increase. In fact, he could have easily followed Louisa home."

"Enough." Mrs. White took a sharp breath. "You've gone from calling him a bum to accusing him of murder."

"She's not wrong." Ally rested her hands on the counter and looked between the three women. "It's possible that he was involved. We can't prove that he wasn't. And you're right, sometimes people end up on the streets because they've done some terrible things in life. We can't simply rule him out because he seems sweet and lost now. But without some kind of motive or evidence, we have no reason to believe he was involved either." She glanced over at her grandmother. "Do you mind if I take off for an hour or two? I want to track down this James Carlo and see if he has anything to say about Tucker. If they used to be partners, maybe Tucker confided something more to him than he has to anyone else."

"It's worth a shot." Charlotte nodded. "But you shouldn't go alone."

"I'll go with you." Mrs. Bing stood up quickly.

As she turned to the front door she gasped. "Oh no, it's starting!"

"Yes!" Mrs. White cheered at the large snowflakes that tumbled down in front of the window. "I was hoping for a snowy Christmas."

"Ugh." Mrs. Cale stood up as well. "I'm going home and staying home until it's all gone!"

"Be careful out there, ladies!" Charlotte called out to them. "Ally, we should salt the sidewalk."

"I'll do it right now." Ally nodded to her grandmother. "Mrs. Bing, are you sure you want to come with me in this weather?"

"I'm sure. I'll just have another cup of coffee while you take care of things." Mrs. Bing turned back to Charlotte and smiled.

Ally tugged a heavy bag of salt out through the front door of the shop. The sidewalk already had a coating of snow on it. She looked up at the sky in time for a few snowflakes to land on her face. Several more swirled behind it. She guessed there would be a few inches on the ground within the hour. If she wanted to have her conversation, she would have to hurry. She spread a thick layer of salt on the sidewalk, then tugged the remainder of the bag back inside.

"Mrs. Bing, are you ready?"

"We should all be on our way." Mrs. Cale buttoned up her coat. "If we don't get home now it will be tough going."

"You're right." Mrs. White waved to Charlotte.

"Do be careful in this mess." Mrs. Cale called out.

"Ally, maybe you should postpone your visit." Charlotte frowned as she looked out through the open door at the fast-falling snow.

"We'll be quick, I promise." Ally grabbed her keys, then gestured for Mrs. Bing to follow her. "It's in Mainbry, but it's on this side of town so it's not very far to drive." She unlocked the doors as they approached the car.

"I'm not afraid of a little snow." Mrs. Bing took off her hat and brushed off the feathers that stuck out of it. "Do you think he will have some information for us?"

"I hope so." Ally started the car. After a quick drive to Mainbry, she spotted the house number of the address she'd found. The house appeared tiny, and a bit rundown. A man stood near the driveway with a snow shovel in his hand. It was snowing much harder in Mainbry, already a few inches had accumulated.

"James?" Ally walked up to him with Mrs. Bing a few steps behind her.

"Who's asking?" He turned to look at her, his face flushed with the cold. Snow hung from his hair that draped down over his forehead.

"My name is Ally. This is my friend." She gestured to Mrs. Bing as she stepped up beside her.

"Mrs. Bing." She offered her hand to the young man.

"No first name?" James smirked as he shook her hand.

"Not one that you need to know." Mrs. Bing pursed her lips.

"I've seen you around." James nodded to Ally.

"Maybe at my shop. I run Charlotte's Chocolate Heaven, in Blue River." Ally looked in the direction of Blue River.

"Your name is Ally, not Charlotte?" James gave a short laugh. "That's odd."

"It is." Ally forced a smile. "My grandmother, Charlotte Sweet, is the one who opened the chocolate shop."

"Oh, I see. I've heard a lot about Charlotte. Everyone seems to know Charlotte." James held up one hand. "All good things I assure you."

"That's wonderful to hear." Ally cleared her

throat. "We're here to ask you a few questions about Tucker. You two were partners, weren't you?" She locked her eyes to his.

"Partners?" James shook his head. "If that's what you can call two kids caught up in a mess." He scraped his snow shovel along the sidewalk, then tossed the load of snow off to the side.

"But you didn't do as much time as Tucker did?" Ally watched him as he scooped up another pile of snow.

"No, I didn't." James tossed the snow.

"Why is that?" Ally narrowed her eyes. "Did you agree to testify against him?"

"No." James tossed the snow shovel down into the pile of snow he'd created. "I didn't get as much time because my mother didn't turn me in with all of the stolen goods. They were in his possession when he was arrested, so he got more time."

"Did Tucker ever mention to you how he felt about his mother?" Ally raised her shoulders in an attempt to shield her neck and cheeks from the cold air that blew past.

"That wench?" James chuckled, then shook his head. "I'll tell you something, if she was my mother, I would have offed her, too."

"Excuse me?" Ally glared at him. "Are you

saying that you think he had something to do with his mother's murder?"

"Isn't that what everybody's saying?" James locked his eyes to hers. "That's what I've been hearing, anyway. And, I stand by what I said. What kind of mother throws her kid to the wolves like that?"

"Maybe she wanted him to learn that his actions have consequences." Ally gritted her teeth to prevent a sharp tone from entering her voice.

"Sure, but that kid was young, and he wasn't ready to handle being in prison." James snatched up the snow shovel again. "And this is life on the outside. No one will hire you. You have to take what gigs you can get. It's not exactly easy. My neighbors are paying me to keep our sidewalk clear, but it won't even be enough to keep the lights on in my house. Tucker is the last thing on my mind. She did that to him, and he didn't handle it well."

"Maybe not, but Louisa was trying to get him a job and she gave him a place to live. I'm sure he saw how much she cared about him." Ally took a step back as the snow shovel scraped across the sidewalk once more.

"Who knows what he saw. Who knows if he

killed his mother. It's none of my concern." James tossed the snow to the side. "All I know is that he had a lot to be angry about. I haven't heard from him since he got out, and I hope it stays that way. Sometimes it's best to leave the past in the past."

Charlotte looked up from the register as Ally stepped back into the shop. She peeled off her snow-covered coat and sighed.

"It didn't go well?" Charlotte raised an eyebrow.

"Unfortunately, he didn't have a lot to say about Tucker, other than that he had good reason to hate his mother."

"Where is Mrs. Bing?"

"I dropped her off at her place. She mentioned that we should spread the word to the shops to keep collecting the donations to ensure that Louisa's efforts don't go to waste." Ally winced. "Mrs. Bing is going to take over and pick up the charity money from the shops."

"That's good." Charlotte smiled. "As long as she isn't alone when she collects the money."

"That's what I told her, and she said she would

speak to the police about escorting her." Ally wrung her hands. "I really need to try to speak to Nancy again and see if we can get the statue back, but if I do she might call the cops on me. I really don't want to get the cops involved if I don't have to. I don't want her son to get into trouble because his mother won't get him to return the statue and get things straightened out."

"I can talk to her." Charlotte shrugged. "There's no bad blood between us."

"Are you sure?" Ally met her eyes. "She might get nasty just because of your relationship to me."

"I can handle that." Charlotte stepped past her and placed a light kiss on her cheek. "But we need more cookies."

"I'll get right on it." Ally nodded, then headed for the back.

Charlotte took off her apron and took a deep breath. She wanted to avoid confrontation with Nancy, but after Ally told her about her son stealing from the shop, she needed to give Nancy the opportunity to make things right and make it clear to the woman that he would not get away with it again.

"Mee-Maw?" Ally stuck her head out of the kitchen.

"Yes?" Charlotte turned to look at her.

"Be careful when you talk to Nancy. It's possible that Cody was involved in the theft from the mail truck. If we go at her too strong, she might clam up entirely. I already learned that lesson." Ally frowned. "See if she has anything to say about where Cody was when the charity money was stolen."

"Okay, I'll see what I can find out." Charlotte glanced towards the front door. "It looks like you're in for quite a crowd. I won't be long." She waved her hand over her shoulder as she held the door for the new customers, then stepped out.

As Charlotte walked in the direction of the jewelry store, she had to trudge through a thick layer of snow. Despite the salt on the ground, the snow continued to pile up. She saw the lights on in the jewelry store and quickened her pace. When she pushed open the door, the woman behind the front counter looked up at her.

"Welcome, Charlotte!" Nancy smiled. "It's good to see you. You must be looking for something special to brave this storm."

"I am." Charlotte smiled as she tugged her scarf loose. "Something to cheer up a friend."

"Oh? The holidays can be so tough for some."

Nancy gestured to an assortment of bracelets. "Does your friend like colored stones? Emeralds?"

"I'm not sure." Charlotte sighed. "She's hard to buy for. She's down about everything that's been happening around here. The murder, and the theft. I can't blame her. It surprises me that no one has been arrested for stealing from the mail truck."

"You should look into that vagabond that's been loitering around town. I've chased him away from my store a few times, but he just keeps coming back." Nancy crossed her arms as she glared in the direction of the large, front window. "I told the police after my robbery, that I thought he was the one who did it. But of course, they didn't do anything about it."

"I'm sorry to hear that." Charlotte's gaze swept across the assortment of sparkling diamonds on display. "It looks like you've replenished your supply."

"These?" Nancy glanced down at the diamonds. "They're not nearly as valuable as the ones that were stolen. They're pretty enough, and that means I'll sell plenty, but I'll still take a loss for the season."

"Didn't your insurance money cover the diamonds?" Charlotte looked up at her. "You did have insurance, didn't you?"

"Of course. Yes, that covers the loss of the diamonds, but I can't replace them in time for the holiday season, which means I lose out on the income I would have made from selling them." Nancy narrowed her eyes as she looked back down at the diamonds in the case. "These will only bring in a quarter of the profit I was expecting."

"I'm sorry to hear that." Charlotte met her eyes. "That must make things difficult for you. You're a single mother, aren't you?"

"Yes, I am. My ex-husband lives on the other side of the state. He has no interest in our son anymore. First, he fought for custody and won, now that he has a new girlfriend, he dumped him on me. So, it's up to me to make sure that he is taken care of, and yes, this was quite a blow for me." Nancy shook her head. "I thought Blue River would be a safe place to open my business, but it doesn't seem that way."

"It really is a great town." Charlotte cringed as she glanced away from her. "I know that's little comfort with what you've been through."

"Oh, I got over the theft, but then to have your granddaughter lie and accuse my son of stealing from her shop?" Nancy shook her head as she glared at her. "That's something I can't tolerate."

"Ally would never lie about something like that." Charlotte took a step back from the counter. "Maybe there was some kind of misunderstanding, but if she says that your son took something from the shop, then that is what she believes happened."

"She may believe it, but that doesn't make it true." Nancy sighed. "I have too much to do. I can't argue about this."

"I have no interest in arguing. I heard about some perfumes that Louisa was going to deliver to you, the day she was killed. Did you receive them?" Charlotte glanced around in search of the perfume that Jen described.

"Some of the perfumes, yes. Apparently, some were damaged along the way." Nancy frowned. "One more thing that went wrong. It is just piling up this season."

"Have you sold them all? I don't see any on display." Charlotte's gaze traveled the shelves again before settling on Nancy.

"I had a lot of online orders." Nancy shrugged. "They were part of a promotion. Free perfume if you spend over a certain amount. I shipped them all out this morning so they will arrive in time for the holiday."

"Oh, well that's good at least." Charlotte smiled

at her. "I do hope that things will begin to get more pleasant for you here in Blue River."

"I suppose your granddaughter is the one who will decide that. Since she has the police in her pocket, I'm guessing she could really cause me some trouble if she wanted to." Nancy looked straight at Charlotte.

"Ally doesn't want to cause you any trouble." Charlotte frowned.

"No trouble?" Nancy glared at Charlotte. "Accusing my son of theft causes trouble."

"Just check his belongings." Charlotte nodded. "He was in the shop looking for a present for you. Maybe he couldn't afford the statue he stole, but he still wanted to give it to you."

"Not a chance." Nancy tipped her head towards the door. "I think you should get going. I doubt that you came here to buy anything at all. You're a spy for your granddaughter, and just like I warned her, if I see you around here again, I will be the one to involve the police."

Charlotte sighed as she took a step back from the counter.

"It doesn't have to be like this. It really doesn't."

"You're right it doesn't, so you and your

granddaughter need to stay out of my business." Nancy pointed to the door.

Charlotte frowned as she walked away. She could tell that Nancy was angry, but was she really in denial about her son? Or was she trying to cover for him?

CHAPTER 14

"I blew it." Charlotte stepped into the shop with a swirl of snow around her.

"What?" Ally hurried over to her with a cup of hot coffee. "You must be freezing."

"It is definitely unpleasant out there." Charlotte shivered, then took the cup of coffee. "I tried to talk to Nancy, but she shut me down pretty fast. She's not going to listen to anything we have to say about her son. Also, Louisa did deliver the perfumes to her, but she already sent all of them out as part of some sort of promotion." She shook her head as she walked behind the counter. "And you're right, she felt off. What kind of mother doesn't want to teach her son that there are consequences for his actions? Unless she really can't believe that he would steal."

"Honestly, part of me wishes I'd never even seen him take the statue. Now, I've made an enemy for both of us." Ally added some candies to the display window. "Unfortunately, I didn't have much more luck with James. I think I'm going to check in with Luke, if that's okay with you? I want to see him and see if he can tell me anything new about the case."

"Ally, Nancy did mention one thing that we might want to consider. She said that she'd seen Rodney loitering outside of her store before it was robbed. She seems to think he might have been involved." Charlotte winced. "I don't know if I believe it, but it seems like he is in the wrong place at the wrong time quite often."

"He seems like such a nice man." Ally frowned. "Maybe, he could steal the money from the mail truck. But I find it hard to believe that he could pull off a jewelry heist. Let alone murder." Her eyes widened. She shook her head. "I just don't see it."

"It's easy to be blinded by compassion." Charlotte put on an apron. "I'm not saying he did it, I'm just saying we need to at least consider it."

"Yes, you're right. And I was just saying the same thing before." Ally headed for the door. "I just hope that it turns out not to be true."

Ally walked towards her car, but the sight of the

snow piled up around it, made her change her mind. Instead, she walked in the direction of the police station. The snow had died down to light flurries that blew in with the wind. She took a moment to savor the sight of the snow. Despite how messy things had become, the pristine blanket of snow gave her a sense of peace. That peace vanished when she reached the police station and stepped into noise and chaos.

"What is going on here?" Ally walked up to the officer at the front desk and left a box of cookies on it. The officers were used to Ally bringing chocolate treats for them.

"Chief is on the warpath." The officer cringed. "He wants both robberies and the murder solved before Christmas."

"Well, I'm sure everyone is doing their best. Does he really think that you don't want the same thing?" Ally rolled her eyes at the thought.

"I think he's hoping that putting the pressure on us will bring up something that we've missed. Thank you for these." The officer pointed at the cookies. "If you're looking for Luke, he's in his office, but he probably won't be there long. We're rounding up suspects."

"Oh? Do you have some new ones?" Ally met his eyes.

"A few. Two criminals from the area that have been caught up in burglaries before, and one homeless man." The officer shrugged. "The usual suspects."

"A homeless man? Are you talking about Rodney?" Ally's heart skipped a beat.

"Yes, I think that's his name. Do you know him?" The officer looked up at her.

"Not really." Ally cleared her throat. "I'll just check in with Luke, I promise I won't keep him long." She walked towards his office. When she reached the door, he was about to step through it.

"Ally." Luke smiled as he looked into her eyes. "It is so good to see you."

"You too. Luke, is it true that you have Rodney here?" Ally smiled and stepped into his office.

"Yes. Why?" Luke followed her back into the office.

"Did you arrest him?" Ally turned around to face him as he closed the door to his office.

"No." Luke crossed his arms as he leaned back against the door. "I just brought him in for questioning. I have reason to believe that he might have some information that I need. How do you suggest I get that from him?"

"Couldn't you have questioned him without sticking him in a cell?" Ally shrugged. "He must be terrified."

"He's in an interrogation room, not a cell." Luke straightened up and crossed the distance between them. "He is dry, and he's warm. Is that so bad?"

"I guess not." Ally smiled slightly. "I'm just worried about him."

"I love that you are." Luke placed his hands on her shoulders. "But I have to do my job, not just for Louisa, but for this whole community. No one is going to feel safe until we find out the whole story about what happened."

"I know." Ally shrugged his hands off her shoulders, then captured one in both of hers. "I'll let you get back to work."

"Thanks." Luke kissed her cheek.

Ally smiled then turned and walked out of his office. Of course, he had a job to do, and that involved questioning anyone that might be suspicious or have information for him.

"How did it go?" Mrs. Bing's eager eyes greeted her as she stepped out of Luke's office.

"What are you doing here, Mrs. Bing?" Ally took a step back in surprise.

"You didn't actually expect me to stay away, did you?" Mrs. Bing laughed. "You do remember that we're in this together, right?"

"I do." Ally smiled.

"Did you find out anything?"

"Only that Rodney is here for questioning." Ally sighed as she glanced down the hallway in the direction of the interrogation rooms. "I hope this is figured out soon."

"With all of us on the case, you know we'll get this all figured out." Mrs. Bing grasped her purse and frowned.

"I think there's something I can do to help Rodney in the meantime." Ally tipped her head towards the door. "Want to join me?"

"Absolutely." Mrs. Bing fished her keys out of her purse, then led the way to her car.

Ally directed her to the area that she had last seen Rodney. She thought about Rodney's small camp in the alley not far from her shop. He had very few possessions, but maybe what he did have had been left behind. Maybe she could ensure that his things were taken care of.

As the car pulled to a stop, she stepped out, and headed for where she had seen Rodney's camp.

"Wait for me!" Mrs. Bing pressed the button on the remote on her keychain to lock the doors to her car.

"It looks like only his cardboard and a few things that look like rubbish are here. He must have taken what was important with him." Ally took a step back when something caught her eye under the corner of some cardboard. "What is that?" She pointed to it.

"It's a perfume bottle." Mrs. Bing nudged it with her foot. "A cheap knock-off it looks like."

"Really?" Ally picked up the bottle. "It's empty." She sniffed the opening. "Yes, definitely a perfume bottle, but that stench, ugh."

"It does stink." Mrs. Bing took a step back. "I wonder where he got it from."

"Maybe the dumpster." Ally peered over the edge of the dumpster. "Look, there's a bunch of them in the dumpster." She pulled herself up farther on the edge of it to get a better look inside. She was relieved that they were both wearing gloves. "How would they have all ended up in here?"

"I don't know, something's not right." Mrs. Bing

grabbed one of the perfume bottles from the top of the dumpster. "Look at this." She turned the bottle upside down. "Completely empty. How strange is that?"

"Something is going on here." Ally sighed. "We need to figure out what it is."

"Do you think he stole them?" Mrs. Bing's eyes widened as she looked at the pile of bottles in the dumpster.

"No, I don't think so." Ally shook her head. "That's the strangest part. Mee-Maw said that Nancy told her they sold out of the perfumes. She said she had shipped them this morning. So, if that's the case, what are the perfumes doing in the dumpster?"

"Clearly, Nancy is lying." Mrs. Bing crossed her arms and shivered. "Oh, it's getting even colder out here, I bet we're in for more snow."

"We might be." Ally looked up at the sky, then looked back at Mrs. Bing. "The question is why would she lie about the perfume being sold? Why would she throw out the perfume in this dumpster, when she has a dumpster right outside of her store? None of it makes sense. Does it?"

"No, it really doesn't." Mrs. Bing started back towards her car. "I'm sorry, Ally, but I have to get out of this cold, my hands are freezing even with gloves on." She shoved her hands into her pockets. "We should go talk to Nancy."

"I'm afraid that's not an option, not unless I want to get arrested myself." Ally quirked an eyebrow as she followed after her. "Which I don't."

"You can't talk to her, but I can." Mrs. Bing smiled. "Why don't we take a drive over?"

"Are you sure, Mrs. Bing? She's pretty combative." Ally frowned.

"You know me, Ally." Mrs. Bing met her eyes with a grin. "You really don't think I can handle it?"

"You're right." Ally smiled as she settled in the passenger seat. "I'll just wait in the car."

"Good." Mrs. Bing drove in the direction of the jewelry store. "At least the streets are starting to clear." She sighed. "It wasn't as big of a mess as we expected."

"Not yet." Ally peered out the window at the brooding sky. "But I'm not convinced that we won't get more."

"It's definitely possible." Mrs. Bing parked in front of the jewelry store. "What do you think I should ask her?"

"Maybe mention that you found the empty perfume containers." Ally met her eyes. "That might rattle her a bit. Tell her you were hoping to buy some. I'm curious how she will react to being caught in a lie."

"I'll find out." Mrs. Bing winked at her, then stepped out of the car. She walked to the door, stopped for a second in front of it, then turned straight back towards the car and hopped back in. "Well, that was a waste of time, there is a 'back in twenty minutes' sign on the door."

"Maybe we should just come back later," Ally suggested. "That way I can go to the shop and help Mee-Maw."

"Okay, I'll take you there and then drop in on a few friends and see if I can find out the latest gossip about all of this."

"Okay, but I'll walk."

"Are you sure?" Mrs. Bing asked.

"Yes, it's not far to walk and the chilly air will wake me up."

"Okay." Mrs. Bing smiled. "We'll catch up later."

Ally stepped out of the car and waved as Mrs. Bing pulled away and drove in the opposite direction. She smiled at the energy and determination the woman had. As she started to walk down the street, she ran over the information she'd gathered in her mind. Out of the corner of her eye, a bright red truck caught her attention. She watched as it rounded a corner and took off faster than the rest of the vehicles that were going slowly because of the snow.

CHAPTER 15

*A*lly's heart raced at the sight of the red truck. She pulled her phone out of her pocket and dialed Luke's number.

"Ally!"

"Is Tucker still in custody?" Ally hurried down the sidewalk and around the corner.

"Yes, why?"

"I just saw his truck." Ally took a sharp breath. "If he's still in custody, who is driving his truck?"

"Are you sure it's his?" A note of disbelief entered his voice.

"I'm pretty sure. There aren't any other trucks that color in this area, at least none that I've seen. I really think it's Tucker's. I'm trying to catch up with it to see who is driving it." Ally told him the street she'd just turned onto.

"Okay, I'll be right there. Are you driving?"

"No, I'm on foot, but the traffic is backed up because of the snow, I might be able to keep up with him." Ally hurried as she caught a glimpse of the truck turning down another street. She gave Luke the names of the streets and the direction the truck was going in.

"Okay, I'll get over there as fast as I can."

"Be careful, Luke, the roads are slippery." Ally frowned as she tucked her phone back into her pocket. She followed the truck into the parking lot of a strip of stores. As she watched, the truck parked. Her heart pounded as she waited for the driver to step out. As the truck door swung open, Luke's car pulled up beside her.

"It's over there." Ally pointed in the direction of the truck, just as the door pulled shut again. "The driver was about to get out, but I guess he changed his mind. Is that Tucker's truck?"

Luke squinted across the parking lot at the truck, then nodded.

"It's the same plate. I'm going to go have a conversation with whoever is driving it."

Ally followed at some distance behind him. She

wanted to see who was in the truck and she didn't want Luke to stop her because she got too close.

When Luke reached the truck, the door swung open, and a man stepped out.

Ally took a sharp breath at the sight of him.

"James!"

"Yeah?" He turned around to face them both. The moment he saw Luke, he held up his hands. "I don't want any trouble, man."

"It's hard for me to believe that when you're driving Tucker's truck." Luke straightened his shoulders as he looked into the other man's eyes. "Do you have an explanation for that?"

"It's Tucker's?" James shrugged. "I had no idea."

"Really? Then how did you come to be driving it?" Luke pulled out his phone and began to make a few notes.

"I found it." James cleared his throat.

"You found it?" Luke narrowed his eyes. "Do you mean you stole it?"

"No, I mean I found it." James sighed. "I knew it was too good to be true. I just thought maybe my luck was turning around."

"What do you mean?" Luke stepped closer to him.

"I found it in my driveway a few days ago. It

was parked, with the keys in it, and a full tank of gas. I knew it wasn't mine, but I needed a vehicle to get around for a few jobs. It seemed like perfect timing. So, I took it for a spin, and when everything ran well, I decided to borrow it. To use it until someone showed up for it." James held out the keys. "I didn't steal it. You can give it back to Tucker if you want."

"I thought you said you didn't have any contact with Tucker?" Luke asked.

"I didn't." James crossed his arms. "Didn't you just hear me? I found the truck in my driveway. I had no idea that it belonged to Tucker."

"That's hard for me to believe." Luke shook his head. "I'm going to speak to Tucker about it, and if he says something different then we're going to have quite a problem."

"Go ahead. Talk to him about it." James glared at Luke. "See if I care." He turned and strode towards the cleaners not far from where he parked the truck.

"You're just going to let him go?" Ally took a sharp breath.

"The truck hasn't been reported stolen." Luke turned to face her. "I can't arrest him just for driving it. But once Tucker confirms that he didn't loan it to him, I can pursue things further."

"How frustrating." Ally balled her hands into fists. "He is certainly up to something. He had to have known this is Tucker's truck."

"I don't doubt that, I just can't prove it, yet." Luke cleared his throat. "Tucker refused to tell us where his truck was, so we haven't been able to search it. Like I said, he seems intent on making himself look guilty. Now that we know James has it, I'm going to try and get a warrant to search it, seeing as we know it was most likely near Louisa's house on the day she was murdered."

"What about Rodney? Did you release him, yet?" Ally walked with him back towards his car.

"I'm afraid I can't do that just yet. There is evidence that he has been stealing." Luke paused beside his car.

"What evidence?" Ally held her breath. She wanted Rodney to be innocent, but part of her wanted an answer more.

"One of the things I found in his possession was this gift card." Luke displayed a picture of the gift card on his phone. "Now, I know people are generous around the holidays, but I can't think of any reason why someone would give Rodney a gift card to a makeup store. Can you?"

"No." Ally frowned as she studied it. "I don't think there's even one of these shops around here."

"My guess right now is that Rodney is the one who broke into the mail truck. He probably took a bunch of mail and found the gift card in one of the envelopes." Luke shrugged as he tucked his phone back into his pocket. "I know that it's not what you want to hear, but it's what I'm going with right now."

"Even if Rodney did steal from the mail truck, that doesn't mean that he killed Louisa." Ally shook her head. "He doesn't look strong enough to me."

"It is possible that he took her by surprise and used a rope to strangle her. Even if he isn't that strong, Louisa would have had a hard time fighting back." Luke winced.

"But he didn't know where she lived, right?" Ally sighed. "I'm grasping at straws."

"Yes, you are. If he followed the mail truck, he could have easily followed her back to her house on foot. It stops frequently and it's not like you can't walk everywhere in Blue River. Maybe she confronted him, maybe she let him know in some way that he was going to be arrested, and so he came after her. I'll need to find the evidence to back it up, but right now that is the best I can come up with. The gift card is a solid start." Luke frowned as he met her eyes. "I know that's not what you want to hear."

"I don't know what I want to hear anymore." Ally sighed as she gazed back at him. "At this point, I just want to know what happened. You have two people in custody that I really don't think committed this crime, but I also don't know who did. I should get back to the shop. Mee-Maw has been covering for me."

"Let me give you a ride." Luke pulled open the passenger door for her.

"No, it's all right. The walk will do me good. It gives me a chance to think." Ally kissed his cheek. "Thanks for coming so quickly. Let me know what Tucker says about the truck."

"I will." Luke pulled her close for a kiss on the lips, then walked back around the car to the driver's seat. He looked across the top of the car. "It's been crazy. I promise to try to get this wrapped up quickly."

"I know." Ally blew him a kiss. "See you later, hopefully."

"I'll do my best." Luke winked at her, then settled in the car.

Ally turned and walked back towards the chocolate shop. With each step she took, her thoughts traveled back to James, and Tucker, and Rodney. Had James stolen Tucker's truck? Had Tucker given it to him for some reason? Where did Rodney fit in? Everything felt off.

As Ally opened the door to the shop, she caught sight of her grandmother leaning over a serving tray of freshly made chocolate crinkle cookies.

"Oh, those smell delicious." Ally walked over, picked a cookie up from the tray and smiled. "I can't resist."

"Neither can I." Charlotte winked at her as she picked up a cookie as well. "How did it go?"

"I'm left with more questions than answers." Ally shook her head as she leaned against the counter. She filled her grandmother in on the details about the truck. Then took a bite of the dense cookie with a crisp coating. She closed her eyes for a second as she savored the rich taste.

"You know what that means, don't you?" Charlotte narrowed her eyes.

"That James stole Tucker's truck?" Ally raised an eyebrow.

"It means that when Mrs. Bing saw Tucker's truck near Louisa's house, it might not have been Tucker that parked it there. It might have been James. The same goes for Rodney witnessing the truck near the mail truck at the time of the theft." Charlotte shrugged. "It's just a possibility, nothing we can prove yet, but it's something, isn't it?"

"It is something." Ally considered it as she tapped her fingertips against the counter. "You said Louisa spilled some perfume on the floor in the library, perfume that was going to Nancy's shop, right?"

"Yes." Charlotte met her eyes. "Why?"

"There's something about those perfumes. It doesn't make sense why they were empty, and that Nancy would throw them all away. She was one of the last people to see Louisa alive, I just feel like we're missing something there. Do you mind if I go speak to Jen? In fact, maybe I should take her some of these cookies." Ally walked around behind the counter and grabbed a box.

"I think that's a great idea. I'm not sure what more she can tell you, but you're right things don't add up with Nancy. Jeff is going to come join me and try his hand at melting chocolate again. He's bringing some jewelry to display as well." Charlotte helped Ally fill the box with cookies. "You should have seen his face light up when I told him he could."

"He should be proud of that beautiful work." Ally quirked an eyebrow. "Just keep a close eye on it."

"I will." Charlotte frowned. "Nancy's son hasn't been in the shop again, but I'm going to watch for him."

"Good. I shouldn't be too long." Ally hurried out the door with the box of cookies in her hand. As she stepped out, she nearly collided with Mrs. Bing. She marveled at how much energy the woman had.

"Ally, I was just coming to touch base. I didn't find out anything new of course. Did you?" Mrs. Bing sniffed the air. "Are those chocolate crinkle cookies?"

"Yes, for Jen." Ally met her eyes. "Do you want to join me? I can update you on the way. I want to ask Jen a few questions about Louisa, and the perfumes she needed to deliver."

As they walked to the library, Ally filled Mrs. Bing in on Luke's theory about Rodney.

"It does make sense. If he found a gift card, he would have kept it." Mrs. Bing pulled open the door to the library.

"Maybe, but if he stole the donation money, why was he still on the streets? Why didn't he treat himself to a hotel or a bus ticket to somewhere warmer?" Ally shook her head. "I don't get it."

"Oh my." Mrs. Bing pinched her nose.

"I know." Ally winced. "New carpet, apparently."

"Ally, Mrs. Bing!" Jen waved to them from her desk. "Good to see you both." Her eyes settled on the box in Ally's hands. "Oh, did you bring me something?" Her eyes widened as she reached her hands out.

"Chocolate crinkle cookies." Ally smiled as she handed them over.

"Yes, yes, yes!" Jen offered a whispered cheer as she grinned. "You just made my day."

"I was hoping to." Ally glanced around the library, then looked back at her. "The snow didn't shut you down?"

"Not yet. But we're supposed to get more tonight. I'm guessing we won't open in the morning." Jen opened the box. "I hope you don't mind, I'm starving?"

"Not at all." Mrs. Bing peered into the box.

"Please, have one." Jen smiled as she held up the box.

"Thank you so much." Mrs. Bing selected a cookie.

"Jen, my grandmother mentioned that Louisa had boxes with her when she stopped in here on her last shift." Ally frowned. "With perfume in them?"

"Oh yes." Jen nodded. "She did."

"Perfume like this?" Mrs. Bing pulled a bottle out of her purse.

Ally's eyes widened.

"I didn't know you kept a bottle."

"Oh, I'd know that smell anywhere." Jen laughed as she scrunched up her nose. "When Louisa dropped that bottle of perfume, I had hoped that it would improve the smell around the library, or at least in that one spot. But it only made things worse. As she was cleaning it up, she and I joked about how terrible it smelled. She was so upset because not only did the perfume bottle break, but the perfume spilled onto an envelope for Nancy as well. It seeped right through the envelope and revealed a gift card." She rolled her eyes. "I told Louisa not to worry about it, but she was so upset that she would have to give it to Nancy in that state."

"There was a gift card in the envelope?" Mrs. Bing's voice raised, drawing the attention of the few people in the library. "Sorry." She blushed and put her finger to her lips.

"Yes, it slipped my mind when Charlotte was here. It was one for that makeup store, Sabrina. It's a pretty popular one these days." Jen gestured to her own bare face. "I'm not a big fan, but I know many people are. Louisa was so upset and I'm sure Nancy was, too. If it wasn't ruined completely it certainly smelled bad from the perfume. It wouldn't surprise me if it wasn't perfume at all. In fact, I kind of hope it wasn't." She shuddered at the thought.

"Interesting." Ally narrowed her eyes as she looked at the bottle in her hand. "So, it's possible that the gift card that Rodney had, was delivered to Nancy along with the perfume bottles that were tossed in the dumpster." She looked over at Mrs. Bing. "Who in their right mind throws away a gift card? It's the same thing as throwing money away."

"I'm not sure." Mrs. Bing shook her head. "I certainly wouldn't."

"I'm not sure what you're talking about." Jen shrugged as she took a bite of her cookie. "But I can't imagine anyone throwing away one of those gift cards. They could easily be resold for cash."

"Interesting. Unless the card was so damaged it was useless," Ally suggested. Luke had never mentioned that the card was too damaged to be used. But maybe he couldn't tell. Ally pursed her lips, then nodded to Jen. "Thanks for your time, Jen, enjoy the cookies."

"I intend to." Jen grinned. "Thanks again."

CHAPTER 16

"*O*h wow, the snow has already started again." Ally pulled the hood up on her coat as she stepped out of the library.

"It's supposed to get bad tonight." Mrs. Bing shivered. "I'm going to get some of that hot spiced cider. Join me?" She looked over at Ally.

"Actually, I think I'm going to check on something with Luke." Ally squinted through the snow. "Enjoy your cider."

"I will, and I'll bring some to Charlotte, too." Mrs. Bing pulled the collar of her coat up around her cheeks and hurried down the sidewalk.

Ally walked towards the police station, her thoughts still focused on the revelation that Rodney was most likely in possession of the same gift card that had been with the perfumes. She needed to get that information to Luke. It might not be enough for him to release Rodney, but at least it would hopefully rule out the idea that he had stolen the gift card from the mail truck.

"Ally?"

She looked up to see Luke just walking up to the door of the police station.

"Luke, just who I came here to see."

"That will always make me smile." Luke opened the door for her. "Let me guess, you've cracked the case?"

"Which one?" Ally sighed. "I'm afraid I've gotten nowhere on the murder. But I did find out that Rodney likely got the gift card out of a dumpster near where he was sleeping, not from the mail truck."

"What makes you think that?" Luke led her into his office.

Ally explained what she had found out from Jen as she sat down in a chair in front of his desk.

"You're saying Nancy threw out a gift card?" Luke frowned as he sat down behind his desk.

"Yes, it looks like it." Ally scooted her chair closer to the desk. "Which makes me wonder if the card was actually worth anything. Maybe it was damaged from the perfume. Did you check the validity of it?"

"Someone is looking into it. Let me see what they have found out." Luke picked up his phone. Ally listened as he spoke, but from the one-sided conversation she had no idea if the validity of the gift card had been determined. He ended the call. "The officer was able to confirm that the card had been canceled because apparently it had been damaged. A new one has been issued."

"Great." Ally sat back in the chair and smiled. "So, that makes it unlikely that Rodney stole it."

"It does." Luke nodded.

"That explains why Nancy had thrown the card out and why Rodney had it. But why did she go all the way across town to another dumpster to throw it and the perfume bottles away?"

"No idea." Luke shook his head. "I am going to ask him about it. Again, he isn't very talkative."

"I think that maybe somehow the robbery there, the robbery of the mail truck, and Louisa's murder are all connected." Ally shrugged as she sat back in her chair. "It's a long shot, I know, but it doesn't hurt to look into it, does it?"

"What makes you even think it's a possibility?" Luke picked up one of the folders on his desk.

"I don't know. Blue River is a quiet, small town, and all of these crimes taking place at once, it just feels like there might be more to the story. I think you should look at the jewelry store robbery again."

"You think I might have missed something?" Luke sat forward as he looked at her.

"I just think that with the new information you have, you might be able to figure out who might have been involved in the robbery." Ally shrugged. "Tucker and his partner James had been released from prison. Now we know James was in possession of Tucker's truck, which he likely stole."

"Actually." Luke shook his head. "Tucker insists that he left the truck in James' driveway, just like James described it. He says the truck wasn't stolen."

"Really?" Ally stared at him. "Unbelievable."

"I'm not saying I believe it, but there's not much I can do about it if he refuses to report it stolen." Luke sighed. "Right now, it's a dead end."

"Maybe not. Maybe even that is a clue." Ally smiled. "Can you tell me more about the robbery at Nancy's store?"

"Sorry, not now. I have to go. I have more interrogations to do." Luke smiled as they both stood up. He gave Ally a hug and a quick kiss on the lips. She immediately felt herself relax in his embrace. Her heart warmed whenever she was in his arms.

"Love you." Ally smiled.

"Love you, too." Luke winked, then he opened the door and they left the office together and walked in opposite directions.

As Ally walked towards the shop, she was relieved that she had hopefully cleared Rodney of the thefts. But she wanted to find out more about the jewelry store robbery.

"Ally?" A familiar voice called out to her.

"Christian." Ally turned around and smiled at Christian Palo, a local reporter and relatively new addition to Blue River. "I haven't seen you for a few days."

"I was on a story in the city. My old boss wanted me to cover it, because his main reporter was out sick." Christian grimaced. "Just my luck that all of the action would happen when I'm away."

"I know." Ally smiled. "Do you have time for a quick coffee and chocolate at the shop."

"No sorry, I don't." Christian shook his head as

he put his hands in his pockets and shivered. "My parents are coming into town for Christmas, so I have to go meet them at my house soon. We'll catch up after the holidays?"

"For sure. Quick question." Ally smiled.

"Yep." Christian nodded.

"You didn't by any chance cover the story when Nancy's jewelry store was robbed?" Ally asked.

"Yes, I covered the story." Christian narrowed his eyes. "Why?"

"Just curious." Ally shrugged. "What can you tell me about it?"

"Not much. I managed to get a peek at the crime scene, and it matched what Nancy told me, which I presume is what she told the police as well."

"What did she say?"

"Nancy was at a town meeting in Mainbry when she got a call from the alarm company, alerting her to a break-in. Witnesses saw a flashlight in the shop. When she arrived at the store, she found that the security bars on one of the windows had been removed and a window had been broken, and all of the display cases were emptied. The safe in the back room had not been opened or tampered with."

"Why did she leave the jewelry in the display cases?" Ally asked incredulously. "If someone went to all the trouble of breaking into the jewelry store, why wouldn't they have tried to get into the safe? If there was a safe, why would Nancy leave her most valuable diamonds vulnerable in the jewelry display cases?"

"She had not locked up that night, her shop assistant, Lola Burnest, had. Nancy had Lola leave the diamonds in the display case. She didn't want Lola to know the code to the safe. Nancy was going to come back to the shop after the town meeting in Mainbry and lock everything up properly, but the shop was robbed before she could."

"Really, didn't you say the alarm went off?"

"Yes, it was only triggered near the end of the robbery. Apparently, only certain areas of the shop are alarmed." Christian shrugged. "The police got there quickly, and the robbers had already fled the scene."

"Anything else?" Ally's mind swam as she tried to piece everything together.

"No, that's it." Christian's phone buzzed with a text. "I'm sorry. I have to go." He waved goodbye as he turned around. "We will catch up soon."

"Thanks. See you soon." Ally waved.

Ally walked past the jewelry store and noticed Lola behind the counter. She thought about going to speak to her, but she decided she wanted to think things through first and she needed to check on how everything was going at the shop. She headed back to the chocolate shop, mulling over what Christian had told her about the robbery.

Ally arrived at Charlotte's Chocolate Heaven in time to see Mrs. Bing and her grandmother clink their cups of cider together.

"Celebrating?" Ally smiled as she pulled off her scarf, then joined them at the counter.

"You should have seen the rush we just had!" Charlotte wiped her forehead and laughed. "Trust me, we earned this celebration."

"Charlotte, there's another batch of candies ready." Jeff stepped out of the kitchen.

"Great, thank you so much." Charlotte smiled at him. "Good job."

"I think I'm getting the hang of it." Jeff nodded to Ally. "It's getting worse out there, huh?"

"I don't think the snowplows are going to be able to keep up." Ally leaned against the counter and shared the information she'd learned from Luke and Christian.

"Do you really think that Tucker just gave his truck to James?" Charlotte narrowed her eyes. "I don't think he would do that."

"I don't think so either." Ally frowned. "But that's the story he told Luke. Tucker's friend Ashley, Polly's daughter, said that Tucker has been acting frightened, and he won't tell the police where he was instead of his parole meeting. If he had a reason to be afraid and he still does, Ashley seemed to believe the reason is James."

"That's definitely possible." Mrs. Bing nodded. "Maybe James wanted to plan some kind of crime with Tucker and tried to force him into it."

"Maybe." Ally sighed. "I hate to think it, but maybe the jewelry store robbery?" She looked between the three of them. "What do you think? Is it too much of a stretch?"

"Actually no." Jeff snapped his fingers. "The pieces fit. Maybe Louisa hadn't worked out who stole the donation money when she spoke to Mrs. Bing and the line cut off, maybe she had worked out who stole the diamonds. Maybe James and Tucker robbed the jewelry store, and Louisa found out about it. Maybe she confronted James or Tucker, maybe one or both of them decided to take care of the problem."

"But if James is the one that killed Louisa, why would Tucker be protecting his mother's killer?" Ally frowned.

"Because he's afraid." Charlotte took a deep breath. "He's afraid that if James killed his mother, that he'd be willing to kill him as well."

"Then the only way to keep Tucker safe might be to get James arrested for the robbery and murder." Ally straightened up. "But we have no evidence that James was involved with the robbery at the jewelry store. We need to have a look inside the store."

"What?" Charlotte narrowed her eyes. "You know neither of us can go near that store again."

"Not while Nancy is there." Ally glanced at the clock on the wall. "I saw Lola at the store, I should go talk to her and see if I can have a look around."

"Ally, I'm not so sure that's a good idea." Jeff frowned. "What if Nancy catches you there?"

"Hopefully, she won't." Ally shrugged.

"Well, you're not going alone. If you want to talk to Lola and have a look around you are not doing that alone and risking someone catching you in there. What if Luke or Nancy catches you?" Charlotte took off her apron. "I'm going with you."

"Mee-Maw, I need you to stay here, the shop

needs to stay open a little while longer as I have some orders that need to be picked up tonight. I know I've asked a lot of you, but if you could do this, I'll have a better chance of finding out what really happened to Louisa." Ally looked at her grandmother pleadingly.

"I'll go." Mrs. Bing stood up from her stool. "I'm not banned from the store."

"Are you sure? I want to come with you in case something happens, but I'll stay outside," Ally said. "I don't want you going there alone."

"Okay." Mrs. Bing nodded. "Let's go, before the storm gets any worse."

"Seriously?" Jeff looked between the three women. "You're going to go through with this?"

"Mrs. Bing is just going to have a look and speak to Lola. It's not a big deal." Ally shrugged, then headed for the door.

"Be careful!" Charlotte called out to her.

CHAPTER 17

$\mathcal{A}$lly ducked her head as she stepped into a barrage of snowflakes. She grabbed Mrs. Bing's hand and steered her through the snow towards the jewelry store.

"The lights are out. I think we might be too late."

"I would love to have had a look around on the inside." Mrs. Bing sighed.

"I know."

"I doubt that the store is going to reopen. The snow is piling up and everyone is closing up early." Mrs. Bing shrugged.

"Maybe it doesn't have to be open."

"But how are we going to get in?" Mrs. Bing followed her around the side of the store. "I mean it's a jewelry store. There is no way she doesn't have an alarm."

"Her alarm only went off near the end of the robbery, so we should have some time. Let's just see if there's anywhere we can get in." Ally tried the side door, then the window beside it. She walked around trying the front door and windows as she walked. The doors were locked and the windows she tried were locked and had bars. She shook her head as she looked at the next one. "They all have security bars."

"What about that one?" Mrs. Bing pointed out another window near the end of the wall. "It looks like it's a bit open."

"You're right it does. That must be the window that the robbers went through because the security bars have been removed." Ally walked over to it and gave it a light shove up. "It's so high up, it's not going to be easy to reach it."

"I can reach it. All you have to do is give me a boost." Mrs. Bing smiled as she pulled off her heavy jacket. "I'm sure I can make it."

"I just don't want you to get hurt." Ally glanced over her shoulder in the direction of the street. The snow continued to fall, and she could no longer see the pavement. "But if we're going to do this, we should do it now, while it's snowing. It might keep people away."

"Okay, let's do it." Mrs. Bing stretched her hands up to the windowsill and grabbed on. "Just a little boost and I'll be in."

"All right." Ally wrapped her arms around Mrs. Bing's legs and tried to lift her. She managed to get her about an inch off the ground before her arms began to burn. "I don't think I can, Mrs. Bing!"

"Hold on, I'm almost there!" Mrs. Bing wiggled her body side to side.

"Mrs. Bing, I can't!" Ally swayed as she tried to keep her in the air.

"Got it!" Mrs. Bing released a heavy sigh.

Ally let go of Mrs. Bing's legs and looked up to see her half in, and half out of the window. Her legs dangled against the wall.

"Mrs. Bing, are you okay?" Ally gulped as she watched the woman continue to wiggle.

"Just fine, I just need a minute." Mrs. Bing grunted and squirmed.

"Are you stuck?" Ally's voice dropped to a whisper.

"No, of course not." Mrs. Bing huffed. "Do be a dear and give me a little push, will you?"

Ally stared at her backside, covered in a maroon

skirt, and wondered exactly where she was supposed to put her hands.

"Maybe you should come back down."

"Don't be foolish. Just give me a shove and I'll be in. Ally, don't be shy, I used to change your diapers!" Mrs. Bing's laughter drifted out from inside the jewelry store.

"You did?" Ally took a sharp breath, then laughed. She placed her hands on Mrs. Bing's backside and gave one firm push.

Mrs. Bing let out a cry, then disappeared through the window.

Ally gasped as she heard a thump.

"Mrs. Bing?" She jumped up in an attempt to see in the window.

"I'm okay. Don't worry. I'll open the side door." Mrs. Bing's voice faded as she hurried away from the window.

Ally grabbed Mrs. Bing's coat and ran over to the side door and held her breath. She waited for the alarm to sound. Surely, it had been tripped by Mrs. Bing's fall. Instead she heard the click of a lock, then the side door opened.

"Voila!" Mrs. Bing straightened her skirt and smiled.

"That was amazing." Ally gave her a quick hug. "Are you sure you're not hurt?"

"Fit as a fiddle." Mrs. Bing brushed her hair back from her eyes. "It was quite an adventure. Now, let's have our look around before we end up in handcuffs."

Ally shuddered at the thought. The handcuffs she could handle, Luke's expression when he saw her behind bars, she could not.

"It stinks in here." Mrs. Bing covered her nose as she opened the door to the office. "I'm not sure I can handle this smell long enough to look through anything. I can't hold my breath that long."

"Let me try." Ally stepped into the office and immediately recognized the smell that permeated the room. It was the perfume. "She must have spilled gallons of that perfume in here." She covered her nose and did her best to get farther into the office. "But I don't see any stains on the carpet."

"Maybe it's that." Mrs. Bing pointed to a large vase in the corner of the room. It had no flowers in it, but plenty of liquid.

"Oh wow, I think you're right." Ally took a whiff of it and winced. "Why would she store all of the perfume in this vase?" She eyed a small net on the table beside it. "She wouldn't have kept a fish in this, I hope."

"No, but she might have used that to fish things out of the vase." Mrs. Bing poked her head into the room a little farther. "But what?"

"I have no idea." Ally backed out of the office, her chest tight from trying to hold her breath in between words. "I'm going to need a gas mask to look through her paperwork."

"Let's look around out here first, where the air is a little clearer." Mrs. Bing led the way into the main area of the shop. "I can't believe the jewelry isn't locked up. Look at all of this beautiful jewelry." She eyed the assortment of jewels inside the glass display cases.

"Don't remind me." Ally took a deep breath of the fresher air. "If we get caught in here, saying we just came in for a look, is not going to be a good enough defense. We have to hurry."

"It would help if we knew exactly what we were looking for." Mrs. Bing glanced over at her. "Any thoughts?"

"I don't know exactly. We know that she threw out the perfumes. We know that she's not telling the whole truth about things. But I still don't see a connection between her and Louisa's death. Why would she want her dead?"

"Oh Ally, look at this." Mrs. Bing picked up a backpack and held it open for Ally to look inside.

"I knew it! I knew that he stole that statue." Ally narrowed her eyes, then reached for the statue. At the last second, she stopped. "No, put it back where it was. If I take the statue back, then she will know we were in the jewelry store."

"Okay, I'll put it back." Mrs. Bing set the backpack down in the corner behind the register. "Cody must spend a lot of time here with his mom."

"Yes, he must." Ally walked behind the counter and looked over the length of it. "There's a duress alarm button here." She pointed out the button. "Don't bump into it or we'll be caught for sure."

"Hm, maybe not." Mrs. Bing pointed to a bit of wire that hung from the button. "It looks like it's been disconnected."

"Disconnected?" Ally's eyes widened. "Why would anyone do that?"

"It might have something to do with the reason why the alarm didn't go off when we came in, and the window was partially open." Mrs. Bing shook her head. "None of this makes sense. Leaving all of this jewelry vulnerable is just ridiculous."

"You're right." Ally crossed her arms as she scanned the room again. "Anyone could just break in and take what they wanted. You would think after having endured one robbery she would be far more cautious."

"You would, wouldn't you." Mrs. Bing nodded. "What if there's more to the story?" She turned to face Ally.

"Like what?" Ally met her eyes.

"What if the jewelry store robbery was a setup?" Mrs. Bing snapped her fingers. "What if the robbery was an inside job. What if Lola set it all up?"

"But Christian said that during the robbery the window had been broken and the missing jewelry was documented. The alarm went off. It didn't seem faked. Nancy was at the town meeting during the robbery and witnesses saw someone with a flashlight in her shop. Oh no!" Ally ducked her head as she caught sight of a flashlight beam flicker through the front window of the shop. "I think we've been spotted."

"We're not going to be able to get back outside fast enough." Mrs. Bing gasped as the light shone through the windows.

"Sh." Ally pulled her closer to her. "Our best defense is a good offense."

"What?" Mrs. Bing stared at her. "Are you saying you want to attack a police officer?"

"No!" Ally winced at the thought. "We just need to pretend that we are supposed to be here. If we can fake it long enough to get out the door we might be able to avoid a big mess."

"How are we going to do that?" Mrs. Bing raised her eyebrows.

"We need to say that we think Peaches went in here. Just follow my lead." Ally stood up from behind the counter. She expected the door to swing open. When the flashlight beam continued past the window, Ally sighed with relief. "I don't think we've been spotted."

Ally walked towards the door with Mrs. Bing close behind her. She slowly opened the side door and peered around outside. When she didn't see anyone in the street, she grabbed Mrs. Bing's hand and they stepped out.

"I think we're in the clear, maybe they were just looking to see if someone was in there. But we should keep moving." Ally and Mrs. Bing hurried towards the chocolate shop.

As Ally reached for the door with Mrs. Bing close behind her, it swung open. Ally took a step back, startled by Luke's presence in the doorway.

"Ally, Mrs. Bing." Luke looked at the two women, then stepped out of the shop. "Where have you two been in the middle of this storm?"

"We wanted to get Christmas presents at the jewelry store, but it was already closed. I am so behind on my shopping," Ally rambled.

"The jewelry store?" Luke stared at her in disbelief.

"Yes." Ally smiled wider. "What are you doing here?"

"I came to drop off the toys and see you." Luke smiled.

"I'll wait inside for you, Ally." Mrs. Bing walked past them and sighed with relief as she entered the shop.

"It's good to see you." Ally hugged Luke.

"And you." Luke looked into her eyes. "But I don't have very long. I have to get back to work."

"Did you look more at the robbery of the jewelry store?" Ally asked.

"I have spent a bit of time on it, but not much, I will look into it more." Luke put his arm around her. "Why?"

"We think something is off about the robbery." Ally smiled at the warmth of his touch.

"You do?"

"Yes, we do. I'm just not sure what yet. I told you, we were suspicious of Nancy. And now we are more suspicious of Lola." Ally narrowed her eyes. "How did the robbers get in so easily? Why did it take so long for the alarm to go off during the first robbery? What were the chances that the place would be robbed when Lola had locked up and the jewelry was in the display cases instead of the safe?"

"So, you don't think it's Nancy, now you think it's Lola?" Luke frowned.

"I don't know. It's just that Nancy's story didn't add up. She ordered these perfumes, she claims she sold out of them as part of a promotion and sent them all out, but we found the empty bottles in a dumpster, why would she lie about that?" Ally frowned. "I can't fit the pieces together, but what if Lola was involved. Nancy was one of the last people to see Louisa alive. But what if Lola also saw her? What if Louisa discovered something that Lola didn't want her to?"

"Like what?" Luke held her hand.

"Mrs. Bing and I have a theory. What if the robbery was an inside job? What if Lola staged it? What if she organized the robbery with James and maybe even Tucker?"

"What if?" Luke shook his head. "Do you have any evidence?"

"No, nothing solid." Ally sighed. "Just a feeling."

"I'll look into it." Luke smiled. "Ally." He looked at her, his eyes narrowed. "Just be careful. This isn't your case to solve."

"I know." Ally hugged him, then headed into the shop as Luke walked towards his car. She was shocked to find a few customers in the shop despite the snowstorm.

"Ally, are you okay?" Mrs. Bing rushed towards her.

"I'm fine." Ally smiled as she walked towards the counter. "We can regroup in the morning." Ally winked at her as she hopped behind the counter to help her grandmother.

After helping her grandmother serve the customers and updating her on the events of the evening, they were both tired by the time the customers cleared out. Charlotte went home with Jeff as Ally finished off for the day.

After closing up the shop, Ally headed home. With the case still on her mind she settled in for a snuggle session with Peaches, while Arnold sprawled out on the floor at her feet. Just talking things through with Peaches always helped her sort things out.

"Peaches, I can't work this out." Ally frowned. "I feel like all of the pieces should fit together, and yet the picture they create doesn't make sense."

Peaches rubbed her cheek against Ally's hand.

"I know, I should just back off, but my instincts tell me I'm onto something." Ally scratched behind the cat's ear. She ran through what she knew so far out loud, so that Peaches could hear, too. "I don't think it's Rodney. Especially now that the gift card has been explained. If I rule out Rodney as the killer, that only leaves Tucker and James. I'll be honest, I want it to be James. He obviously did something to squeeze Tucker. But Tucker's mother betrayed him once by turning him into the police, if he thought she was about to do it again, he really did have the best motive. But what about Lola? Was she really involved in the robbery? Could she also have been involved in the murder?" She stretched her arms above her head and yawned. "Maybe things will be clearer in the morning."

CHAPTER 18

*A*lly woke up the next morning to a cat nose against her nose.

"Ah, Peaches!" Ally opened her eyes and ducked back. "Am I late to feed you?" She glanced at the clock.

Peaches meowed and crawled around her head on her pillow.

"No, I'm not late. You just think I need to get back to work, huh?" Ally smiled as she pet the cat. "And you're right. It's time to find out the truth once and for all. What better way to try to find out the truth, than to just ask?"

Despite the snow the night before, the streets were fairly clear as Ally headed in the direction of the shop. She was relieved to see the lights on in the jewelry store. She wasn't sure if it would be open, yet. She parked her car, then walked straight to the jewelry store. As she reached the door, she reached for the handle in the same moment that Mrs. Bing did.

"Mrs. Bing, you have to stay out of this." Ally stared into her eyes. "This is dangerous now. We know that Lola might have done something illegal, no that doesn't make her a killer, but there's a good chance she, or someone related to the crime, is. You have to stay away from the jewelry store."

"You're not." Mrs. Bing narrowed her eyes. "We need to see if we can find more clues and evidence inside that shop. We can't just let her get away with this."

"I know, but we have to be careful." Ally nodded.

"What if we talk to Nancy about our suspicions?" Mrs. Bing asked.

"I thought about that, but after accusing her son of stealing and seeing her reaction I think it would be better to try and get evidence before we tell her our suspicions about Lola. Also, she might be hiding something as well. Those empty perfume bottles just don't make sense." Ally grimaced. "I'm sure that Luke is working on the search warrant for the store.

We should stay out of this, at least at the moment." She took a deep breath as Mrs. Bing started for the door again.

"You stay here, I'll call if I run into any trouble." Mrs. Bing waved her hand.

"Mrs. Bing." Ally groaned, then followed after her. "Wait."

"Why?" Mrs. Bing spun around to face her, the feathers in her hat swung wildly above her head. "Why should I wait? Louisa was a good friend of mine, she was a decent and generous human being. She was murdered, and I'm not going to give the person who might have been involved in her murder, the chance to fly the coop. I get it, you have your whole life ahead of you, and you don't want to land up in jail, but I am not you, Ally. My years are getting shorter, and that makes me think about what I might want to use them for. There is not a single thing that I find to be more important than using what time I have, the same time that was stolen from Louisa, to make sure that her killer and any accomplices are put behind bars."

"Mrs. Bing." Ally wrapped her arms around her and frowned. "I'm so sorry. I know this has all been incredibly difficult for you."

"If you knew that, you wouldn't ask me to leave

it alone." Mrs. Bing pulled away from her. "Ally, I'm not asking you to help me. I would never do that. What you have with Luke is beautiful, and your grandmother would certainly have my hide if she knew we were even talking about this. I'm just asking that you not try to stop me. Don't tip off Luke about what I'm up to. Can you do that for me, please?"

"I'm sorry but I can't." Ally shuddered as she made a decision that she knew would likely lead to chaos in her life.

"So, you're going to turn me in?" Mrs. Bing pursed her lips. "I never thought you would really do that."

"No, I'm not going to turn you in. I'm just not going to let you go in alone." Ally wrapped her hand around the door handle. "There's a right way to do things, and a wrong way, Mrs. Bing. You and I will figure this out together. If we play this right, we'll be able to get the evidence to give to Luke and get out of the store without causing any trouble."

"I'm not sure that's possible." Mrs. Bing raised an eyebrow. "But I will follow your lead."

"Good." Ally pulled the door open to the shop and peered inside.

Nancy stood behind the counter with her back

to the counter, and her hands deep in a large zippered bag.

"Welcome to our sunrise sale!" Nancy called out without turning around.

"I'm so glad you're already open." Ally smiled as she stepped farther into the shop.

"You." Nancy turned to face her, then frowned. "I thought you were warned not to come around here anymore. Do I need to call the police?"

"Oh, please don't." Ally grimaced as she clutched her hands together in front of her. "It will ruin the surprise."

"The surprise?" Nancy glared at Ally. "Are you playing some kind of game here?"

"Not at all. I'm here to apologize, and also, ask for your help." Ally paused in front of the counter and peered down through the glass. "The gift I had planned for Luke has fallen through. Now I'm stuck with what feels like only hours before Christmas. I was hoping that you would have something here that might work, but when it comes to Luke's taste in jewelry, well he doesn't have any." She laughed as she glanced up at Nancy. "I brought my friend Mrs. Bing to help me choose. So, do you think you can help me, or is it hopeless?"

"I haven't heard the apology part yet." Nancy crossed her arms as she studied her.

"Oh, you're right." Ally straightened up and looked into her eyes. "I am so sorry for accusing your son. Obviously, it was a misunderstanding. He's really a good boy, and I shouldn't have ever questioned you about him. With all the chaos of the holiday, sometimes things just get mixed up."

"I can understand that." Nancy sighed. "It's been crazy here, too. But theft is a sensitive point for me. After my shop was robbed, you should expect that."

"You're absolutely right, and I'm so sorry for any pain that I caused you." Ally lifted her eyebrows as she smiled. "Any chance you can come to my rescue? I was thinking maybe a nice watch, maybe with a few diamonds in it? But I'm not sure. My budget is pretty tight."

"I did just get a new shipment of watches in." Nancy took a step back from the counter, then looked up at the clock. "But it's a pain to put them all out."

"Oh, you don't have to put them out if you don't want. You can just show me where they are. I will pick one fast, I promise." Ally met Nancy's eyes. "It would help me out so much if you would let me just have a look."

"All right fine." Nancy rolled her eyes then led them both down the hallway. "They're in the vault." She typed a few numbers into the keypad, then the door swung open. "Let's have a look." She gestured for Ally and Mrs. Bing to step inside.

"Thanks so much." Ally grinned as she stepped into the vault.

Mrs. Bing stepped in behind her.

"You know, I have installed some new cameras since the robbery." Nancy smiled as she lingered by the door of the vault. "Hidden ones."

"Oh?" Ally turned to face her as her heart began to race.

"Let me save you some time. Yes, they were running last night." Nancy locked her eyes to Ally's. "I've heard of small towns being full of nosy people, but you two?" She looked between them. "You just took it to another level, didn't you?"

"We were looking for Ally's cat." Mrs. Bing cleared her throat.

"Sure." Nancy smirked.

"We wanted to speak to you about Lola staging the robbery." Ally blurted out. She knew that they had been caught snooping and wanted to find out if Nancy knew that Lola had set up the robbery.

"Lola?" Nancy laughed slightly. "You think that

Lola could have pulled this off?" She shook her head. "I think you two have learned a little too much about me, and my business."

"No." Ally started to realize her mistake. Maybe Lola wasn't involved? Maybe it was all Nancy? But why? "Not at all." Her chest tightened.

"It's too late for denials. I have connections of my own, and I know that your boyfriend is suspicious of the robbery. He has been working to get a warrant to search my business, my home, and even my car." Nancy stepped closer to the door. "I already know what he's going to find. Luckily for me, I have a backup plan. I'm leaving the state. I'm moving from Mainbry. I'm going to close down the store. That's the reason for my sunrise sale. I thought I'd offload as much as I could while I packed up. But since you two showed up, I guess I'll have to make things happen faster. I really appreciate the effort you've put in, delivering yourselves to me."

Ally noticed Mrs. Bing staring at the vase through the open vault door.

"You were fishing the diamonds out!" Mrs. Bing exclaimed.

"What?" Ally scrunched up her nose.

"There was no robbery. You were fishing the

diamonds out of the liquid in the vase." Mrs. Bing smiled with pride as she stared at Nancy. "I read about this in one of my favorite crime novels. A jewelry store faked a robbery in order to collect the insurance money on their jewels." She frowned. "If the insurance company covers the loss of the jewels, you would have that money as well as the jewels." She stared at Nancy.

"Of course." Ally's eyes widened.

"You doubled your money." Mrs. Bing glared at Nancy.

"You worked it out, Mrs. Bing." Nancy clapped her hands slowly. "Clever you."

"This isn't just about insurance fraud, is it?" Ally stared at her as the pieces started to fall into place.

"It started out that way. I had an acquaintance that would fake a theft, steal my diamonds, and mail them back to me so we wouldn't be seen together and raise suspicion. I set it up so that Lola would close up the shop, so there was an excuse for the diamonds being in the display cases and she would corroborate my story that they were in there. Breaking into a vault is harder to fake. I disarmed the duress alarm in case the robber accidently triggered it, but it would look like it was disarmed by him. Lola's alarm code only arms certain areas of the shop. I told the thief which areas were armed and all he had to do was break in, steal the diamonds, trigger the alarm and escape."

"An acquaintance?" Mrs. Bing wrung her hands. "James?"

"Yes." Nancy nodded. "I've known him his whole life. His parents used to live down the street from me."

"The diamonds were in the perfume bottles?" Ally asked.

"Yes. He sent the perfume bottles with the diamonds in them back to me, so we weren't seen together. It would have been perfect if that incompetent postal worker hadn't broken one of the bottles. We had them delivered over a couple of days. Just in case. James followed Louisa to make sure they were delivered, so he saw Louisa break the bottle. We thought she would just run off with the diamonds, but she didn't realize what was in the bottle at first and brought it to me."

"That's why he was behind the mail truck when the charity money was stolen." Ally's eyes widened.

"Probably. He was following Louisa." Nancy nodded. "He replaced the perfume with a thicker liquid to keep the diamonds hidden."

"Clever plan." Mrs. Bing shook her head in amazement.

"It was." Nancy smirked. "But it didn't all go to plan. When Louisa brought the broken perfume bottle to the shop, she put it down on the counter and the diamonds fell out. She didn't say anything, but I knew she noticed them. Her eyes widened. She looked at me with a knowing look then ran out of the shop. I knew she had to be suspicious that something was up, and she would work it out. Or at least tell someone who would work it out. I couldn't risk it. So, I tried to get my guy to take care of the problem." Nancy rolled her eyes. "But he chickened out of course."

"James." Ally took a sharp breath. "You sent James."

"That's right. I tried to send him to clean up this mess, but he wouldn't go through with it. He refused to go. I had to take care of the problem myself." Nancy shrugged.

"Why was he in the area later in the day?" Mrs. Bing asked.

"He must have got a guilty conscience because he didn't do anything to protect her. He went to check on Louisa. She was already dead by then of course. I knew he could never say anything. If he did, he risked his involvement in the robbery being revealed and he would never see the outside of a jail cell because of his prior convictions." Nancy crossed her arms. "I managed to stop Louisa just as she was about to tell you everything." She looked at Mrs. Bing. "I knew she would turn me in. She'd turned her own son in after all. So, she had to go." She shrugged. "I couldn't risk my freedom and I can't risk it now. I have to take care of myself." She stepped back through the vault door and began to swing it closed.

"Don't do this, Nancy!" Ally stared at her with wide eyes. "You can't do this. We're not going to survive in here very long!"

"Oh, I know that." Nancy continued to close the heavy door. "It was your choice to get in the middle of this, not mine."

"No!" Ally let out a shriek as she tried to shove the door back open. Despite her attempts, the door continued to swing closed, until it latched. Frozen with fear, Ally held her breath as she heard additional locks engage. They were shrouded in darkness.

"Ally?" Mrs. Bing shivered, her body pressed back into the corner of the safe. "Can you get it open? You have a plan, right?"

Ally pushed her hands against the door. The cold metal under her palms offered no hint of giving way. Her heartbeat quickened as her mind began to race. A safe was not meant to hold people. It was meant to be impenetrable. Which meant that air probably couldn't get in either. Her stomach twisted as she recalled the confidence in Nancy's eyes as she agreed that they wouldn't survive long inside the safe. How long did they have? A few hours? One? Even less? The safe wasn't very large. Ally switched on the torch on her cell phone and looked along the ceiling for any sign of an air vent. Instead she noticed the seamless flow of the walls into the ceiling. There was no way out. They were trapped in a steel box.

"Ally?" Mrs. Bing took a step towards her. "What's your plan?"

"Just give me a second." Ally spun in a slow circle, searching for anything that might give her hope. But every inch of the safe appeared to be inescapable. "I'm sorry, Mrs. Bing." She paused in front of her. "I don't have a plan."

"What?" Mrs. Bing's eyes widened. "But you have to. You're so smart. You always figure things out!"

"Not this time." Ally lowered her eyes as panic

bubbled up within her. "We're trapped. I have no idea how to get out, and no one knows we're here!"

"Someone must have seen us go in." Mrs. Bing rushed up to the door and began to pound on it.

"Don't hurt your hands, Mrs. Bing!" Ally winced as she saw the force Mrs. Bing applied to the door. "It's several inches thick, no one will hear you pounding. Besides, the store is closed now." Ally sank down to her knees as reality began to settle over her. She'd made a huge mistake, and not only that, she'd allowed Mrs. Bing to be in danger, too.

"She's going to get away with it, isn't she?" Mrs. Bing turned to face Ally. "She's going to get away with killing three people."

"I hope not." Ally bit into her bottom lip, then took a breath. "Luke will wonder where I am. He will call you, and when he can't reach you, then he will suspect we came here, and he will stop at nothing to find us."

"Call! Why didn't I think of that?" Mrs. Bing laughed as she dug in her purse. "We'll just call someone to get us out."

"I don't think your phone is going to work in here. Mine doesn't." Ally frowned as she showed Mrs. Bing her phone. "The metal is too thick."

"Oh dear." Mrs. Bing held her phone in the air above her head. "You're right. I don't have any signal."

"We just have to sit tight and wait for Luke to come and find us." Ally willed her racing heartbeat to slow. "We just have to stay calm."

"Calm?" Mrs. Bing looked around the safe. "Do you think I can't tell this is a sealed vault? How much oxygen do you think we have in here?"

"I don't know." Ally's muscles tensed as she resisted the urge to pound on the door herself. "But we're going to get out of here, Mrs. Bing, we have to stay focused."

"How?" Mrs. Bing walked around the perimeter of the safe. "Is there some secret passageway I don't know about?"

"Try to stay calm." Ally looked into her eyes. She needed to hear those words as much as Mrs. Bing did.

CHAPTER 19

Charlotte stared at the closed sign on the door of the chocolate shop. She looked towards the parking lot, where Ally's car was parked. After dialing her number one more time, Charlotte drove over to the police station, and headed right inside the lobby. She stopped in front of the front desk and looked straight at the officer.

"I need to speak to Luke, now."

"He's a little busy." The officer frowned.

"Now," Charlotte repeated.

"Charlotte?" Luke stepped out of a hallway and walked towards her. "Is everything okay?"

"Ally is missing, I can't reach her." Charlotte stood in front of Luke and blocked his way.

"For how long?" Luke frowned as he tried to ignore the buzzing of his phone.

"I'm not sure. I haven't heard from her at all this morning." Charlotte sighed. "Something is wrong, Luke."

"I'm sorry, but that's not very long. Don't you think she could just be busy at the shop?" Luke glanced at his phone, then looked up at her again. "I'm sorry I'm getting a lot of calls that need my attention."

"You're not listening to me." Charlotte stepped in front of him again, her chest tight with frustration, and the tone of her voice barely restrained. "Something is wrong. I went to the cottage with Jeff because the snow had calmed down, so he could take Arnold and Peaches for a walk and try out their new snowshoes. But she wasn't there. I went by the shop, and it was locked when it should have been open. I looked inside, and nothing has been set up for the morning, even though Ally's car is parked there."

"Maybe she needed to go somewhere, and she walked?" Luke took a slight step back as he studied her. "I know that you're very protective of her, but you should consider that she might have just needed a break."

"Do you really think that I don't know that?" Charlotte glared at him as she stepped closer to him. "Now you listen to me, young man, I've been trying to be polite because I know how much my granddaughter loves you, and I consider you to be family, but if you don't get on that phone and do whatever you have to do to find Ally, then you will discover just how impolite I can be!"

"Charlotte, I'm just trying to rule out all of the possibilities." Luke narrowed his eyes.

"There are no other possibilities." Charlotte shook her head. "I am standing right here telling you that she is missing! That doesn't concern you?"

"Of course it does!" Luke stared back at her. "If Ally is in trouble, I will stop at nothing to make sure she comes home safe, you should know that." He pulled his phone out of his pocket and dialed it.

"Are you calling her cell phone?" Charlotte rolled her eyes. "You don't think I've tried that?"

"No." Luke locked his eyes to hers as he waited on the phone line. "I'm placing a call, so the officers know to look for her and see if she's been spotted anywhere." He turned away from her to speak into the phone.

Charlotte's phone rang. For a split-second she

hoped it was Ally. Her heart sank when she saw it was Jeff.

Charlotte answered, hoping he had seen or heard from Ally, but he hadn't. She explained what was happening.

"Take a breath," Jeff said gently. "Luke's looking into it now. Okay? Just try to remember your own health."

"My health?" Charlotte's voice rose. "Jeff, if anything has happened to Ally, my health is the last thing on my mind. She is my heart and soul. I can't lose her."

"Keep me updated."

"I will." Charlotte ended the call.

"Charlotte." Luke pushed past her towards the door. "I've got a tip. I'm going to go check it out."

"I'm coming with you." Charlotte followed quickly after him.

"Maybe it would be best if you stayed here." Luke paused long enough to glance back at her.

Charlotte stared hard into his eyes, her determination pounding through her veins.

"Okay, okay, let's go." Luke gestured for her to follow him.

"Oh Luke, there you are!" Mrs. White and Mrs.

Cale met them at the front door. "You have to help us. Mrs. Bing is missing!"

"What?" Luke stared at them.

"All morning, I haven't been able to reach her." Mrs. White shook her head. "It's not like her. We always say good morning to each other."

"The two of them." Luke shook his head, then headed for his car. "I'm going to find them both."

"Not without me!" Charlotte opened the passenger side door.

"Or me!" Mrs. White pulled open the rear passenger door.

"Or me!" Mrs. Cale opened the rear driver's side door.

"Fine! Just get in!" Luke rolled his eyes as he started the car. He drove quickly towards the jewelry store. "An officer saw her a few hours ago near the jewelry store. My guess is they went in there together."

"But it's closed." Charlotte frowned as she stepped out of the car.

"But it might have been open a few hours ago." Luke walked towards the door.

A pig and a cat walked around the corner towards Charlotte.

"Jeff." Charlotte smiled slightly.

"I saw the commotion." Jeff frowned as he held the leashes.

Luke narrowed his eyes as he tried the door. "It's locked."

"Then bust it down!" Mrs. White huffed. "What are you waiting for?"

"I can't just break down a door." Luke shook his head. "The three of you have to calm down or stay in the car."

Peaches lunged for the door. She pounced on a long feather that wafted in the cool wind, its stem stuck in the crack of the door.

"Stand back, I'm breaking it down!" Luke hurried back to his car and pulled out a crowbar.

"Luke!" Charlotte gasped, then corralled the other women, Jeff and the animals out of the way as Luke slammed the crowbar into the door. It started to splinter. He hit it again and again as the door continued to break, until there was an opening big enough for him to step through.

"Stay here!" Luke barked the command as he drew his weapon and ducked through the door. "Ally?"

Charlotte shooed Mrs. White and Mrs. Cale back to the car.

Arnold squealed frantically and tried to tug Jeff into the shop. His squealing grew more frantic.

Charlotte crept into the shop after Luke. Arnold tugged hard at his leash.

"Charlotte, wait!" Jeff called out as he followed the pets into the store.

"Ally? Mrs. Bing? Are you in here?" Luke headed towards the back of the shop.

Charlotte followed after him. When she bumped into a display, the sound startled Luke. Luke spun around to face her, his gun pointed at her for a split-second.

"Charlotte! Don't sneak up on me! What were you thinking?"

"Are they back there?" Charlotte tried to peer past him into the back room.

"No one is." Luke sighed as he holstered his gun. "We were wrong, they're not in here." He started to turn away. Arnold lunged past Luke into the back room and straight to the vault door. Jeff held tightly to his leash but let him lead the way.

"Wait." Charlotte grabbed Luke's arm.

Arnold squealed and scratched at the bottom of the door. Peaches joined in.

"They are telling us something. They must be in the safe." Charlotte pointed at the safe.

"Ally?" Luke walked up to the vault door. "Mrs. Bing, are you in there?"

Arnold kept squealing and Peaches scratched harder at the door.

"Luke, they are in there!" Charlotte insisted.

"I'm going to have to get some help. But I don't know how I'm going to explain that we think they are in there because of a pig and a cat." Luke pulled out his phone. "We have to find someone who can get in the vault, we'll never be able to bust into it."

"But how long will that take?" Charlotte gasped. "Can they breathe in there?"

"I know the code." A boy stepped through the broken door.

"Cody?" Charlotte looked at him with wide eyes.

"You have to hurry, my mother is looking for me." Cody clutched his backpack. "I was here when Ally and Mrs. Bing came in this morning. But I ran off when I heard my mother shut them in the vault. She won't leave town without me."

"The code." Luke pointed to the keypad on the door. "Can you put it in?"

"Yes." Cody hurried over to the door and pressed the buttons. Seconds later, the door released.

"Oh, thank goodness!" Mrs. Bing hurried out with a flourish of her arms. "It's so muggy in there!"

"Are you okay?" Charlotte caught her hands. "Did she hurt you?"

"I'm okay." Mrs. Bing sighed. "But there's a murderer on the loose!"

"Ally?" Luke peered inside the vault.

"Luke!" Ally flung her arms around him. "How did you find us? How did you know we were here?"

"Actually, Peaches pounced on a feather in the door." Luke smiled as he looked over his shoulder at Mrs. Bing. "I recognized it from your hat. That's when I knew that the two of you had to be inside the store. Then Arnold lead Jeff to the safe." He looked at the animals. "They were the ones that found you."

"Thank you, my clever little friends." Ally bent down to pat Arnold and Peaches who were nestled close to Charlotte. She stood back up and smiled at Luke.

"I'm just so relieved you're safe." Luke looked into her eyes.

"Me too." Ally looked over at Cody. "Where's your mother, Cody?"

"She's probably organizing another robbery with James. He was supposed to break in again last night and steal some more jewelry, but you two got in the way. They wanted to make it look like the same thieves had come back to steal more before the window had been repaired and the bars replaced." Cody shoved his hands in his pockets and looked down at his feet. "I'm sorry for stealing the statue. I just thought maybe if I could give my mother something nice, maybe she wouldn't do so many bad things."

"What about the money from the mail truck?" Ally met his eyes. "Did you steal it?

"I did, I just wanted my mother to stop." Cody frowned. "But she didn't care. She said it wasn't enough." He opened his backpack and pulled out the zippered pouch. "Please don't arrest me, I'll give it back."

"No one's arresting you." Ally wrapped her arms around him, then shot a pleading look at Luke.

"It's all right, bud." Luke put his hand on Cody's shoulder. "You did the right thing. You saved two lives. We're going to get you the help you need, all right?"

"All right." Cody sighed. "Here." He handed over his phone. "You might be able to find her with this. I've been tracking her phone for a while to try to figure out what she was up to."

"Thanks Cody." Luke took off through the door of the shop.

Charlotte held her hand out to Cody.

"Come with me, let's get you some hot apple cider."

"Really?" Cody looked up at her with wide eyes.

"Really." Charlotte looked at Ally. "I think we're going to need an extra seat at the table this Christmas."

"Absolutely." Ally smiled. "Hey Cody, have you ever met a pig before?"

"No." Cody smiled at Arnold as he patted him and nuzzled his hand. "He's so cute."

"Well, it looks like you're going to be spending Christmas with one." Ally gave him a light pat on the shoulder.

It certainly wouldn't fix everything in his life, but she hoped it would be a start.

CHAPTER 20

a few days later, as Ally grabbed the plates from the cupboard her phone rang. She put down the plates and looked at her phone to see it was Mrs. Bing calling. She answered straight away.

"Mrs. Bing?"

"Ally, I have to talk quickly I am in the middle of dinner," Mrs. Bing whispered. "I'm hiding in the bathroom. If Mrs. Cale and Mrs. White find out that I have called for an update instead of sitting at the table talking to them, they will not be happy. I have been with them all day and I just had to sneak out and see if you got the latest from Luke."

"Okay, Mrs. Bing." Ally smiled to herself. "You

know that Nancy and James were arrested. What else do you want to know?"

"Everything. Why did James have Tucker's truck?" Mrs. Bing asked quickly. "Why did he miss his parole meeting?"

"Tucker admitted that he'd given James his truck because he tried to force him into helping Nancy with the theft of the diamonds. He didn't want to be involved and he agreed to leave him alone if he gave him his truck," Ally explained. "Tucker couldn't tell Luke where he was when he missed his parole meeting because he was with James. James had cornered him, trying to get him to be his alibi for another robbery he was planning. He wouldn't let him go until after he agreed to be his alibi. By the time he did, he had missed his meeting with his parole officer."

"So, Tucker wasn't involved in the jewelry store robbery at all?" Mrs. Bing asked.

"No, Tucker wanted to stay out of everything. He was worried that he missed his parole meeting, so he went to be alone at the river. He didn't want to face his mother and explain that he had stuffed up his parole." Ally's voice wavered some.

"But why didn't he just go to the police?" Mrs. Bing asked.

"He was too scared. James threatened Tucker and told him he would hurt him and his mother if he didn't help him." Ally sighed. "James blamed Tucker because he had landed up in jail because Louisa turned Tucker into the police."

"Of course, I didn't think of that." Mrs. Bing's voice raised slightly. "Anything else? I have to go back soon. They'll come looking for me in a minute."

"Tucker suspected that James was somehow involved in his mother's murder, but he was too scared of him to tell the police. James was the ringleader when they did the first robbery together." Ally spoke quickly. "Tucker had given up. He blamed himself for his mother's murder because in his eyes if he had turned James in, and explained what Nancy and James were planning before they robbed the jewelry store, none of this would have happened. His mother would have still been alive."

"Oh, of course." Mrs. Bing's voice raised. "He was too scared to turn James in for the robbery and he blamed himself for his mother's murder, so he thought the best thing to do would be to go to jail for his mother's murder."

"Exactly!" Ally agreed.

"Do we know who was in the house when I discovered Louisa on the couch?" Mrs. Bing's voice cracked. "Or did I just imagine that someone was there?"

"No, you didn't imagine it. Tucker was in the house," Ally said. "He found Louisa's body shortly before you arrived. He didn't call the police straight away because he was worried that he would be accused of the murder. He left before the police came."

"Oh, that explains that." Mrs. Bing sighed. "I thought I might have been hearing things. Is there anything else I need to know?"

"No, that's it." Ally smiled. Mrs. Bing was just as inquisitive as she was.

"I better get back before they miss me," Mrs. Bing said softly. "Merry Christmas, Ally."

"Merry Christmas, Mrs. Bing." Ally smiled as she ended the call and picked the plates up again.

As Ally put the plates on the table, she heard Arnold squeal.

"Don't get him too excited, Cody." She laughed.

"It's Peaches." Cody called out from the living room. "She keeps swatting his tail."

"That I believe." Ally grinned.

"Where do you want the rolls, Ally?" A man held out a bowl full of bread rolls to Ally.

"Anywhere is fine, Rodney, if you can find a

space." Ally smiled at the man who set the rolls down in the last empty space on the table.

It had been a tough season, with robbery, murder, too much snow, and too little time. But as Ally watched everyone gather around the table, her heart warmed at the sight.

A knock on the door drew Luke from his position at the stove.

"I'll get it." He opened the front door, and Tucker and Robin stood in the doorway.

"I hope we're not too late. I brought some cookies." Tucker laughed as Arnold ran over to greet his new friends.

"You're right on time." Luke smiled as he led them to the table.

Ally took her grandmother's hand and smiled as Jeff sat down with them. Luke caught Ally's eyes from across the table and winked at her. Her heart warmed at the love she saw in his eyes and she felt for him. Maybe things weren't perfect, but in that moment, they were just right.

The End

WAGGING TAIL COZY MYSTERIES

Murder at Pawprint Creek (prequel)

Murder at Pooch Park

Murder at the Pet Boutique

A Merry Murder at St. Bernard Cabins

Murder at the Dog Training Academy

Murder at Corgi Country Club

A Merry Murder on Ruff Road

DUNE HOUSE COZY MYSTERIES

Seaside Secrets

Boats and Bad Guys

Treasured History

Hidden Hideaways

Dodgy Dealings

Suspects and Surprises

Ruffled Feathers

A Fishy Discovery

Danger in the Depths

Celebrities and Chaos

Pups, Pilots and Peril

Tides, Trails and Trouble

Racing and Robberies

Athletes and Alibis

Manuscripts and Deadly Motives

Pelicans, Pier and Poison

Sand, Sea and a Skeleton

NUTS ABOUT NUTS COZY MYSTERIES

A Tough Case to Crack

A Seed of Doubt

Roasted Peanuts and Peril

Chestnuts, Camping and Culprits

DONUT TRUCK COZY MYSTERIES

Deadly Deals and Donuts

Fatal Festive Donuts

Bunny Donuts and a Body

Strawberry Donuts and Scandal

Frosted Donuts and Fatal Falls

SAGE GARDENS COZY MYSTERIES

Birthdays Can Be Deadly

Money Can Be Deadly

Trust Can Be Deadly

Ties Can Be Deadly

Rocks Can Be Deadly

Jewelry Can Be Deadly

Numbers Can Be Deadly

Memories Can Be Deadly

Paintings Can Be Deadly

Snow Can Be Deadly

Tea Can Be Deadly

Greed Can Be Deadly

Clutter Can Be Deadly

BEKKI THE BEAUTICIAN COZY MYSTERIES

Hairspray and Homicide

A Dyed Blonde and a Dead Body

Mascara and Murder

Pageant and Poison

Conditioner and a Corpse

Mistletoe, Makeup and Murder

Hairpin, Hair Dryer and Homicide

Blush, a Bride and a Body

Shampoo and a Stiff

Cosmetics, a Cruise and a Killer

Lipstick, a Long Iron and Lifeless

Camping, Concealer and Criminals

Treated and Dyed

A Wrinkle-Free Murder

A MACARON PATISSERIE COZY MYSTERY SERIES

Sifting for Suspects

Recipes and Revenge

Mansions, Macarons and Murder

HEAVENLY HIGHLAND INN COZY MYSTERIES

Murdering the Roses

Dead in the Daisies

Killing the Carnations

Drowning the Daffodils

WENDY THE WEDDING PLANNER COZY MYSTERIES

ABOUT THE AUTHOR

Cindy Bell is a USA Today and Wall Street Journal Bestselling Author. She is the author of the cozy mystery series Wagging Tail, Donut Truck, Dune House, Sage Gardens, Chocolate Centered, Macaron Patisserie, Nuts about Nuts, Bekki the Beautician, Heavenly Highland Inn and Wendy the Wedding Planner.

Cindy has always loved reading, but it is only recently that she has discovered her passion for writing romantic cozy mysteries. She loves walking along the beach thinking of the next adventure her characters can embark on.

You can sign up for her newsletter so you are notified of her latest releases at http://www.cindybellbooks.com.

CHOCOLATE CRINKLE COOKIE RECIPE

Ingredients:

4 ounces semi-sweet chocolate

1/2 stick butter

1 cup all-purpose flour

1 teaspoon baking powder

1/2 cup unsweetened cocoa powder

1/2 cup superfine sugar

1/2 cup brown sugar

2 eggs

1 teaspoon vanilla extract

1/3 cup granulated sugar

1/3 cup confectioners' sugar

Preparation:

Makes about 24 chocolate crinkle cookies.

Melt the chocolate, preferably in a double-boiler, and leave aside to cool.

Melt the butter, preferably in a double-boiler, and leave aside to cool.

In a bowl sift together the flour, baking powder and cocoa powder.

In another bowl beat together the melted butter with the superfine and brown sugars until combined. Beat in the eggs and vanilla extract until fluffy.

Gradually add the dry ingredients to the wet ingredients. Mix until well-combined.

Wrap the dough in plastic wrap and place in the refrigerator for at least 3 hours because the mixture will be too wet to roll into balls.

When you are ready to bake the cookies remove the dough from the refrigerator and let sit for about 20 minutes until soft enough to form into balls.

Preheat the oven to 350 degrees Fahrenheit. Line two baking sheets with parchment paper.

Place the granulated sugar in one bowl and the confectioners' sugar in another bowl.

Roll the dough into balls of about one tablespoon in size. Roll in the granulated sugar and then the confectioners' sugar. Place the balls on the baking sheets, leaving about 2 inches between them as they will spread.

Bake in the preheated oven for 10-14 minutes. The cookies are ready when the surface cracks. They will be very soft but will firm up as they cool.

Remove from the oven and leave aside to cool for about five minutes, then place on cooling racks to cool completely.

Enjoy!!

Printed in Great Britain
by Amazon

25541944R00145